Drifter's Gold

Drifter's Gold

WILLIAM E. VANCE

DOUBLEDAY & COMPANY, INC.
GARDEN CITY, NEW YORK
1979

F —
Western

All of the characters in this book are fictitious, and any
resemblance to actual persons, living or dead, is purely
coincidental.

Library of Congress Cataloging in Publication Data

Vance, William E
Drifter's gold.

(A Double D western)
I. Title.
PZ4.V222Dr   [PS3572.A425]   813'.5'2

ISBN: 0-385-14240-4
Library of Congress Catalog Card Number 78-3260

TO
*Kathy and Her Generation of Young Aspiring Writers
with admiration and in appreciation*

Drifter's Gold

Jared Kane stopped the black gelding a hundred yards from the water hole called Simon's Lake. He no longer lounged in the saddle. His leaned-out body was alert. He scanned the desolate land as the pack mule strained at the lead rope, wanting to get to the water. Kane and his animals had traveled two days without water.

The Painted Desert of northeastern Arizona is an awesome country, bordered on the east by multicolored mesas and buttes and on the west by the little Colorado River. Shifting sands of yellow, red, magenta, brown and mauve, and bizarre sand sculptures, make this a beautiful but forbidding land. There is little water to be found and then only by the desert-wise traveler.

Aloft, black buzzards wheeled and glided over the water hole. Kane looked back in the direction from which he had come. Nothing moved in his eyesight except an occasional wave of sand and dust raised by the hot gusting wind. The pack mule brayed piteously.

Facing ahead, Kane kept the black at a slow walk toward the water hole, a hollowed-out space in the colored rock, collecting water from a tiny trickle that came from God only knew where. The little clump of sparse growth around the water was the only green Kane had encountered since entering the desert from the north. The black pumped his head up and down, impatient to get a drink. Kane quieted him with a word. The mule brayed again, tugging on the lead rope.

There were buzzards on the ground, more aggressive than those aloft. Kane's approach caused them to hop awkwardly away, flapping to become airborne. He watched them thoughtfully as the birds lifted high, circling hungrily. Wary, he scanned the spindly brush and hot rocks surrounding the water.

Something dead there, he thought; *or something dying*.

A bundle of rags stirred beside the water hole. The black snorted and Kane felt the animal's muscles tense under his legs. The horse, responding to the reins, stopped but the pack mule surged ahead, pulling on the lead rope. An incoherent babble came from the man.

Kane slacked the reins, rode closer. Drawing his saddle gun from the boot, he stepped to the ground. The black whickered softly, wanting to go ahead to the water. Kane dropped the reins, ground-tying the black, and with his left hand wrapped the pack mule's lead rope around the saddle horn. He was still alert, ready for anything.

He had to have water to go on but he heeded the warning of the time and country. A careless man died young and before his time here.

The sun beat down unmercifully. The wind blew steadily, except for occasional gusts, from out of the southwest, hot and drying, yet cooling his body sweat. His shadow lay black on the sand beside him. The rich blue of the desert high-country sky was free of clouds except for elongated patches over a distant range of mountains. Nothing moved in his sight and only the soft flap of the vultures' wings broke the utter silence of the desert.

He wet his lips and went forward, the rifle now cocked and ready, moving without haste, a big man in his early thirties with an impassive lean brown face and watchful blue eyes. He stopped again, leaning forward. The man didn't move. But it was a man, Kane knew, and there seemed to be no one else around. He stood there, looking at the shallow swale containing the green-rimmed water hole.

Dry grass and a few scrubby trees with withered limbs grew here, or managed to survive. The silence of the desert prevailed.

Kane walked forward, letting the hammer down with care and shouldering the Winchester. A clawlike hand raised from the bundle of rags and dropped weakly. Kane stood over the man, watching impassively. Then he walked around the man and leaned his rifle against a gray boulder, noting a scatter of expended brass shells glittering in the sun on the sandy ground.

Kane walked to the man and knelt beside him. The man's eyes opened, gummy-lidded, red-rimmed, staring wildly. A spasm crossed his dirty bearded face and he exposed broken, yellow teeth in a caricature of a grin as he grabbed Kane's arm. "Somebody come," he croaked. "I knowed somebody would come."

The stink of the man was revolting and Kane rose.

"Oh, God'lmighty don't leave me!" the scarecrow screeched. "Don't go, man, don't go—I kin make you a rich man, I kin! An' I will if'n you—"

"I was meaning to help you," Kane said.

The man relaxed, closing his eyes. His lips moved but no sound came out. He appeared to be offering up a prayer of thanks. That's what Kane thought before he got to know Foulard.

Kane examined the man despite his stench. He found no wounds or broken bones. The man quivered when a hidden buzzard flapped into the air beyond the rocks. His ankle was swollen, the flesh dark beneath the grime. Foulard's gaunt face and emaciated body suggested starvation.

Foulard, sitting up, improved amazingly with a half a can of tomatoes and a piece of jerky in his belly. He looked hungrily at the remainder of tomatoes in the can and belched. While Kane squatted nearby Foulard talked.

"Been here most a month, I figger. Et one lizard." He squeezed his eyes shut, his mouth slack at the memory.

Kane jingled the empty brass shells he'd collected from one hand to the other. "What'd you shoot at?"

Foulard opened his eyes. "Tried to shoot jackrabbits," he said. "Didn't hit ary a one. They quit comin' after a spell. 'Til my shells all gone. Then it seemed to me they knowed it. They'd sit and laugh at me, I swa'r t' God. I near went crazy. Finally got so weak I couldn't even throw rocks at 'em. . . . Then them buzzards come . . ."

Kane filled his two-gallon water bag. He brought the black and the pack mule in to drink. He fashioned a shelter from his tarp to shield Foulard from the blazing sun, preparing to camp there until the man could travel. He kept a sharp lookout over his back trail as he worked. He'd noticed movement earlier in the day. Outlaws, he thought; or Indians.

By the end of the third day of eating, sleeping and talking, Foulard was able to hobble around with the help of a stick Kane cut for him. They were lowering the water level of the tiny water hole appreciably. Kane was impatient to move on, even though he had no definite goal in mind. By that time Foulard had told and retold his story. He, too, was riding south when his horse stepped into a gopher hole, fell and broke a leg and had to be shot. He'd made it to Simon's Lake, thinking his ankle was broken. Turned out to be a bad sprain but he'd almost died of thirst walking into the water hole.

"Drank myself sick," he said. "Then near starved to death. Nobody come. I was scairt, believe me."

"I believe you," Kane said.

"Sure do thank you. Like I said, I kin make it worth your while, Kane."

"I don't expect any payment."

"Man alive, I mean it!" Foulard said, his eyes wide and staring. He raised his voice. "I know where there's a gold cache'll make yore eyes bug out."

Kane was silent, waiting.

"I was on my way to get it when I—I hit a streak o' bad luck. But the gold's there, Kane, an' I'll cut you in on it."

"I'm not interested," Kane said mildly.

"You think I'm loco, I betcha," Foulard said. "I'm not. I kin make you a rich man."

Kane looked at Foulard and saw a wolfish-faced man, ragged and dirty but with a blazing light in his pale eyes. Kane shook his head in disbelief.

"You're makin' a big mistake, Kane, maybe the biggest in a lifetime. In a week or two you could be a rich man."

"If I can get my horse and pack mule to good grass I'll feel rich," Kane said. "They're thinning out and there's a long way to go." He looked over the back trail for a long time and then glanced at Foulard. "What do you need to get this pot of gold you're talking about?"

Foulard licked his lips and scrubbed his face with a shaky hand. "Why, I got nothin' but what you're lookin' at. I need everythin' to get to where I'm goin'."

"We can't stay here any longer," Kane said. He nodded toward the water hole. "That'll be dry in another day. And I'm out of feed for the animals."

Foulard stared at him.

"I'll split my pack between my horse and the mule. I'll help you to where you can buy yourself a horse or rig."

"With what?" Foulard whined. "I'm plumb broke, ain't got a penny to my name."

Kane didn't answer but went to work dividing his

belongings into two piles, planning what would go where, to make a place for Foulard to ride.

"I wisht I could get you to listen to me," Foulard said. "I'm tellin' you true, man, honest-to-God truth. There was this old man, Pete Trawler—"

"Was?"

"Yeah. He's dead now. But he give me this here map on his deathbed."

"I've heard that before."

"But this here is for real." Foulard was almost in tears as he told Kane his story. Pete Trawler was one of the breed of men who drifted west after the Civil War. Fell in with a bunch of outlaws and in their forays had burned a Mexican village. According to Foulard, Trawler had saved one family, one of the ruling dons. In gratitude Trawler had been rewarded with the secret of the gold left by Spanish priests when they had to flee during an Indian uprising. The gold was there, waiting for almost two hundred years.

"All the dons I've heard about wouldn't give away anything," Kane observed. "Not even to one who had saved their lives."

"I know right where it's buried, under an old church," Foulard said desperately. "You help me get it and we'll split right down the middle."

"How'd you get the map?"

"I took care of ol' Pete. He was dyin' and knowed it. He didn't have nobody, no relatives. So he give it to me."

"Why didn't Trawler get the gold for himself?"

"That's easy, he was trapped, that's what. The other outlaws, the gang he rode with, they didn't know about the gold. They would of killed him if he'd tried to leave. Them outlaws killed and looted all along the border, both sides. Trawler was finally captured and stood trial for

murder, sent to Yuma for life. He got sick and was dyin'
and they paroled him. I had a lil' place up the river from
the prison and I took him in, took keer o' him. Pete died
in my cabin on the Colorado River. He give me the map
before he cashed in."

"Now all you got to do is go there and pick it up and
haul it away?"

Foulard didn't meet his look, glancing away. "That's
about the size of it." He stood on his bad leg and winced.
"You goin' someplace in particular?"

"I'm a drifter," Jared Kane said.

Foulard studied him intently. "I've met a lot o'
drifters," he said shrewdly. "You don't look like any I've
knowed."

"You can't tell much about a horse from the saddle on
its back."

"Yeah, maybe not. What d' you say, Kane. Want to give
it a whirl?"

Kane didn't answer at once. He'd been on the move for
more than a year, trying to rid his mind of bitter memories. He winced, thinking about it. Taking on a partner, as
disreputable as this one appeared, could make it easier for
him to forget some of the past, erase painful thoughts.
"I'll think about it, Foulard," he said.

Foulard showed his disappointment. "Ain't likely you'll
get another chance like this," he said sulkily.

"I'll get you to this place where your gold is and then
I'll decide."

"Armijo. New Mex Territory. North o' Santa Fe."

"I'll get you there."

"Gimmie some shells for my gun."

"I've only enough for myself."

"Aw, shoot," Foulard muttered. But he didn't press the
matter.

They traveled by the light of a full moon, letting the animals walk. They moved through the night, the horse hoofs muffled in the sand. Leather creaked and bridle chains rattled. Near dawn they made a fireless camp and slept for two hours and then went on. Foulard's impatience grew and he babbled incessantly about the gold. Looking ahead, Kane had the feeling he wouldn't be able to tolerate Foulard much longer. Stopping at a rise in the ground, he twisted in the saddle and looked over the back trail.

"You do a lot o' lookin' over yore shoulder," Foulard said.

Kane didn't answer, scanning the horizon for movement, a puff of dust. He couldn't see anything in all that vast expanse but he knew someone was out there.

Thinking about it, Kane tried to recapture the feeling of that summer when he was six years old and he'd traveled with his father, John Kane, from Salt Lake City on the narrow gauge that ended in Richfield.

Bishop Garnett and his daughter Christine waited for them in the four-passenger surrey, pulled by two nice-looking grays. He remembered his pa hefting the big canvas bag of tools he used as a stonemason. John Kane had been hired to build a church for the Mormons in the little town of Garnettville, just seven miles from Richfield. He and his pa rode in the back seat, and Christine (she must have been about nineteen or twenty then) twisted around in the front seat and smiled and charmed his pa. They were married even before the church was finished, his pa and Christine Garnett.

Feeling a sudden chill, he spoke to his black and rode on, not looking at Foulard, shutting his chatter out with a conscious effort.

The Garnett brand, one of the biggest between the Rockies and the Sierra Nevada Range; not even Bishop Garnett knew how many cows he owned, nor the number of sheep in the grass-rich untimbered hills surrounding the thousands of acres under Garnett control. . . .

Kane had figured four days to get out of the desert. Three days out of Simon's Lake he fed the last of the grain to the horse and mule, dividing it evenly. On the fourth day, Kane and Foulard had a sip of water and gave the rest to the animals. Kane knew then he'd made a planning mistake.

Ahead of them in the misty distances the mountains appeared like some enormous slumbering beast. As they traveled steadily the outline seemed unchanged, or even receding.

Late in the afternoon of the fifth day a spot of green appeared in the colorful distance. Kane turned in that direction. It turned out to be a dry water hole.

Kane squatted on the edge of the water hole while Foulard scrambled down from the mule muttering, "Oh, lordy, what we gonna do now?"

Kane stepped down into the empty bed and began pulling sand and gravel aside. The soil grew moist as he pulled aside the stones, pebbles and sand. He dug with his hands to a depth of two feet and stepped back, watching the slow trickle of muddy water fill the basin.

It took an hour for the hole to fill, and after drinking and allowing Foulard to quench his thirst, he let the horse and then the mule finish it off.

They traveled on through the night, resting now and then because the horse and mule were weakened. By dawn it was clear that the worst part of the desert was behind them. All around them lay reddish-yellow flat-topped buttes gashed with dry canyons. Many miles lay ahead, though, before they reached Armijo—and the padre's gold.

"I get my hands on all that gold I'm never gonna see another desert," Foulard declared. "I'm gonna live like a king."

"Wait'll you get it in your hand."

"I'll get it," Foulard said and lapsed into silence.

When even the mule began faltering, Kane began looking for a place to rest. He finally found one, a grassy glade among the rocks, with a water seep and some forage, dry brown grass sparsely scattered, which the animals began nibbling hungrily.

"Let's camp here," Kane said. "Just enough water for the horse and mule. See if you can find a few sticks of wood for a fire."

He stepped to the ground and began unsaddling the black as the animals cropped hungrily.

"Let's keep goin'," Foulard argued. "More and better water and graze ahead, som'ers."

"What's the hurry?"

"You know what the hurry is."

"The gold's been there a couple of hundred years," Kane said. "It'll wait awhile longer. If it's there."

He heard the mule move away as he stripped the saddle from the horse's sweaty back and began working his fingers through the damp hair. He turned swiftly when he heard the sound of a horse, picking up his rifle as he turned. Two riders stopped their horses on the incline leading into the glade when he swung all the way around to face them.

"Which way you headed, stranger?" the older of the two men asked, folding his hands on his saddle horn. His pistol was in easy reach.

"Nowhere right now," Kane said.

"Which way you come from?"

Kane looked at the speaker, seeing a medium-sized man, bulky through the shoulders. He shoved back his hat, revealing a broad forehead sloping sharply to a narrow chin. He wore dark clothing and carried a Colt in a brass-studded belt.

"North," Kane said. "Who wants to know?"

"I'm Zack Morton. I work for Hugh Giles."

"Name isn't familiar," Kane said.

Morton's pale gray eyes flickered as he studied Kane.

"Hell with this, Zack," the young, yellow-haired giant with Morton said in a voice of disgust, reaching for and drawing his pistol. "I—"

"Hold it right there," Kane said and cocked the rifle. He felt his heartbeat quicken and blood pounded in his ears as he curbed his rising anger.

Zack Morton licked his lips, a strange feeling coming over him. "You know what you're gettin' into?"

"I can kill one of you before I'm dead," Kane said, his voice almost gentle. "The question is, which one of you will it be?"

"Listen—"

"I can't listen when I'm being pushed."

The younger man's breath whistled out. "I can take him, Zack, just nod—"

"Shut up, Bud," Zack Morton said roughly. He looked at Kane, frowning, as if undecided about something and not knowing what to do about it. "All right, mister," he said softly. "Put away your gun, Bud, real, real easy, and let's get the hell out of here."

Bud obeyed, his face dark with fury.

Morton leaned toward Kane. "I'd like to inquire what your name is, stranger," he said in a placating voice.

"You're not being polite," Kane said.

Morton, hard-eyed but soft-voiced, nodded. "I had a feeling about askin' but I had to do it." He neck-reined his horse around, swiveling his head, keeping his hot, angry eyes on Kane. Then the two of them rode away, quickly, disappearing almost at once around a red-brown outcropping.

Kane rubbed the back of his neck thoughtfully. Hearing a sound behind him, he whirled. Foulard stood beside a great boulder, holding the mule's lead rope. He had gathered a few sticks of wood which he'd secured to the pack. "Hell fire n' damnation! You sure backed Zack Morton down. An' that wild kid, too!"

"Why didn't you tell me someone was on your trail?" Kane demanded, a hint of anger in his voice.

"Hell, man, I thought they was trailin' you."

"Do you think they'd have left peaceably if they'd been after me?"

"Well, I sure don't know what they'd want with me," Foulard said.

"If you're hiding anything else from me you'd better spit it out now," Kane said.

Foulard shook his head. "I don't know what you're talkin' about, I swear," he whined. His face brightened. "You sure bluffed them two off. That kid—he's Bud Giles, old Hugh's son. An' you bluffed them both!"

"What makes you think I was bluffing?"

Foulard only looked at him blankly.

"You want to camp here a spell?"

"Uh-uh. Them two been trailin' us—"

"You, not me."

"Well, all right, but I don't know what for. They'll wait out there and shoot us from ambush."

"You want to go on?"

Foulard nodded eagerly. "Hugh Giles wasn't with 'em. I reckon they just accidental-like stumbled on us. Like as not they think you're travelin' alone."

"Maybe," Kane said reflectively. He realized suddenly that he wanted to keep traveling. He also realized, with discomfort, that Foulard's gold was becoming more and more important to him. Could it be that he was getting the gold fever like so many others before him? He shook his head impatiently in silent denial. "All right, then, we'll keep going but you stay here 'til dark. I'll go ahead and stop when it gets full dark. No moon tonight—"

"Oh, hell, I don't want to stay behind."

"I don't want those two to know you're with me."

"I don't either but I don't wanna stay here by myself. I'll tell you what, I'll stay out of sight. We'll wait right here until it gets dark and then travel." He paused and added, "Lemme have your rifle and I'll fix it so they won't be trackin' us."

"You won't back-shoot anybody with my gun," Kane said.

"They'd shoot us if they got the chance," Foulard muttered.

Kane didn't answer but busied himself with making a fire. Foulard remained out of sight while Kane prepared a meal of beans, bacon, flapjacks and coffee. All his provisions were gone except flour and coffee.

Kane carried a plate to Foulard and then returned and ate his own portion, squatting by the fire, watching the entrance to the small circular valley. While he watched, the stars came out and night came down. The wind died away and there was a silence in the land, broken only by the soft cropping sound as the black grazed the sparse grass.

Kane packed after full night fell. He was ready to go

while Foulard fumbled with the mule's pack. Kane picked up his rifle. "I'll take a look around while you finish." Without waiting for an answer, he walked away from the tiny campfire. In the darkness, out of sight of the campfire, his eyes quickly adjusted to the night. He stood there looking in the direction Zack Morton and young Giles had ridden away. A coyote howled in the distance, a sudden sound ending on a high sharp note. Nothing moved out there that he could see. If the two men were still around, he thought, they'd probably be holed up in a nearby canyon. They didn't appear to be the type of men who'd give up at the first high water. He wheeled and a dark shape hurtled out of the night at him.

He fell backward, warding off the slash of a knife with a savage upward thrust of the rifle. His assailant, smelling strongly of sweat and rancid animal fat, swung upward with the knife and Kane jammed the rifle against the man's throat. With a gurgle the man fell on the sand, writhing. Kane hit the man with the butt of his rifle and stilled all movement.

He scratched a match aflame and knelt in the sand. An Indian, with greasy black hair circled with a red band, blood flowing from around the head band, lay inert, the knife still held loosely in splayed fingers. Kane placed his fingers over the Indian's carotid and felt no pulse.

Shaking out the match, he dropped it and went toward the sound of Foulard's voice calling.

Kane came swiftly to the dying fire and laid his rifle on his saddle and straightened. "I just killed an Indian brave," he said. "Apache, I think."

Foulard stared at him wide-eyed and then looked fearfully out into the night. "You're funnin'," he said.

"No. Go see for yourself."

Foulard stepped closer to the fire. "I'll take your word for it. What d' we do now?"

"Do those men—Morton and Giles—know where Armijo is located?"

"Oh, the hell with them two. I'm worrit now about Injuns."

"You didn't answer my question."

"Nobody put Pete Trawler an' me knowed about Armijo. You're the first I've mentioned it to."

"Now, tell me about Hugh Giles."

Foulard was silent for a long time and then he sighed. "Listen, Kane, Giles is a manhunter, first of all. He used to be head guard at Yuma Territorial Prison. A lot of men in that hellhole was put there by him personally. So he left prison work and took up manhuntin'."

"Why is he after you?"

"I don't know he's after me," Foulard whined. "He just might think I'm somebody else. I'm just guessin'."

"All right, Foulard," Kane said quietly, swinging up on the black. "Let's move on. We'll try to lose 'em, head out up the next canyon and turn north."

"That's not the way," Foulard objected.

"That's the idea. When we travel far enough north to throw them off, we'll find some rocky ground and peel off to the east."

"I see. Well, I sure'n hell hope it works."

"So do I," Kane said. "So do I."

CHAPTER 2

It was two hours after first light when young Bud Giles found his father's camp. He waited in silence while Hugh Giles finished skinning out a spike buck which he let hang to the lower limb of a cottonwood tree along the creek.

Hugh Giles walked away from the deer and seated himself beside a smoldering fire while he whetted his knife. He looked critically at Bud's horse, head drooping from exhaustion.

"When you gonna learn to take care of your horse?"

Young Giles shrugged. "I use 'em the only way I know."

"One of these days—" He broke off, put away his knife and whetstone. "What'd you find?"

"He latched onto some drifter at Simon's Lake. Travelin' east. Zack is keepin' 'em in sight 'til you get there."

Hugh Giles, a brown-faced man, with graying hair, chuckled deep in his throat. "Get yourself a bite to eat and we'll get on after him."

"Why don't you trust me to do it for you?"

Hugh Giles's almost invisible eyebrows went up a notch. "Foulard's my meat," he said. "He lied to me, cheated me, double-crossed me. No, I'm going after him, Bud. Go on, bite off a chunk of that deer meat."

"I don't like meat too fresh," Bud said. "I'm ready when you are."

"Then let's get on with it."

Far away, to the south and east, Nantana, the leader of the Warm Springs Apache, looked stonily at the brave his scouts had brought to his camp. The dead man was one of his best men, now dead of a broken neck, a crushed thorax.

"We will send his spirit to consult with our fathers who have gone before us," Nantana said, and instructed his braves, the nucleus of his attack force still in the forming stage, in preparation of the body for a ritualistic burial. While Nantana talked he fingered the blue medallion hanging by a thin golden chain around his neck. The medallion was a potent charm and Nantana knew his braves were aware of its unfailing powers.

When the ritual was done, Nantana mounted his horse and waved his braves in the direction the men who had killed his friend and bravest warrior had gone.

CHAPTER 3

Far up the canyon Kane stopped the black gelding, twist-ing about in his saddle to watch flickering light bounce off the walls of rock far below: their dying campfire. The mule nudged his leg.

"We're wastin' our time," Foulard complained.

"We'll see," Kane said.

A yellow light flared above them and the thunderous sound of a big-bore rifle crashed in the narrow confines and bounced back and forth between the rock walls. The mule squealed as Kane yanked his rifle from the boot and shot at the muzzle flash. He slipped to the ground, trying to quiet his frightened horse. He stood close to the horse, clucking softly.

"Oh, my God," Foulard whispered. "I told you to gim-mie shells for my gun—"

"Be quiet," Kane said. "How bad is the mule?"

"Thinkin' about a goddamned mule," Foulard mut-tered. His remaining words were lost in another roar of a gun and a muzzle flash of yellow light from above. Kane fired at the flash and heard a faint cry, but the slug hit a rock and whined off into space.

"Got 'im!" Foulard whispered.

"Stung by a rock chip."

"How'd they get up above us?" Foulard whispered in a hoarse, injured voice.

"That's a big-bore rifle," Kane said. "My guess, it's an Indian with one of them Buffalo rifles."

"Injuns? Everybody knows they don't get out nights."

"Old liars' tales," Kane said. "Take the horse and mule and move on up the canyon. I'll keep firing at the rimrock. I'll catch up with you later." He shoved fresh cartridges into the chamber of his carbine.

"I ain't gonna do it," Foulard whined. "Not a single ca'tridge and you expect me—"

"Take my Colt," Kane said, passing the pistol to Foulard. "Get moving now!"

"An' a handful o' shells, Kane."

"No. Go when I start shooting." He raised his rifle and nestled his cheek against the warm stock. He fired slowly and methodically, raking the rimrock above, the bullets singing off the rocks with a vicious whine. He emptied the rifle and moved a few feet away, reloading as he went. A bowstring twanged from the rimrock and an arrow danced along the rocky canyon floor.

Kane waited patiently, listening, looking. A bird called and he suspected it to be an imitation. Wondering why he'd not seen an outline of a man skylighted above, he concluded there must be a shelf of rock below the rim.

He used a string of buckskin he carried in his pocket to hang his rifle around his neck. He went forward without making a sound, by moving carefully and deliberately, putting each foot down before setting his full weight on it.

The big bore thundered again and he felt something tug at his arm. He leaped upward, fingers and feet clawing at the nearly sheer wall, unmindful now of any noise he might make. He found a hold with his left hand and right foot and clung there for a moment and then scrambled upward. A dark outline of head and shoulders loomed above and he got the carbine in his free left hand, thumbed back the hammer and pulled the trigger. With an ear-splitting screech the man tumbled down into Kane and they fell together in a tangle on the rocky trail below. Kane's rifle clattered away as he felt the savage pull of buckskin thong before it parted. He had his knife out but but the man under him didn't move.

He saw the glint of the carbine and picked it up. The harsh crash of his Colt .44 reached him. Foulard had run into trouble, he thought, smelling gunpowder smoke but seeing nothing but darkness and the shine of stars overhead.

Kane stripped off the foot covering of the dead man, a moccasin legging with fringe and beading, which he stuffed inside his shirt. Keeping close to the rocky wall on his left, he followed the upward slope, keeping his rifle ready.

A dozen yards up the canyon he stopped and explored the face rock, finding hand and foot holds by feel. He climbed slowly and quietly until he reached the shelf from which the ambush had been launched. He knelt there in the darkness, holding his carbine, trying to pierce the darkness below. He could see nothing. No sound reached him.

He waited, patient, his senses tuned to the night. Minutes dragged on but he felt no urge to move. Kane had been in trouble before and he'd learned the hard way that it paid to move slowly and with caution. He'd always taken risks but not foolhardy ones.

A faint sound came to him, a mere whisper of buckskin on rock, and a faint outline, almost merging with the night. He smothered the cocking click of his rifle by depressing the trigger as he drew the hammer back with his thumb. He fired by simply letting the hammer go, hearing the solid thunk of the bullet as it went true, feeling the deadly strike in his very hands and insides. Kane moved silently away from where he'd fired the shot.

"Come on here!" Foulard bawled in a panic-stricken voice from upcanyon, his voice echoing between the rock walls. "Kane, where are you?"

Kane went carefully along the rock shelf until he heard the sound of Foulard, the snuffle of the horse below him. "Shut your fool mouth," he called softly.

"I'm spooked," Foulard answered. "Let's get the hell outta here quick."

"What'd you shoot at?"

"Dunno yet. But I got 'im. An' I got his horse."

"That's three. I believe that's all of them."

"Well, come on down and let's get outta here. This damn place gives me the shivers."

Kane descended into the blackness and scrambled to the narrow canyon floor. Foulard stood there holding three animals. The Indian pony, small and wiry, was restless. Kane spoke to it but it wouldn't be quieted.

"Let me have my handgun," Kane said as he reloaded the carbine.

"Lemme keep it," Foulard said. "We might run into more o' them red devils."

Kane held out his hand. "My Colt, Foulard."

"Aw, shoot," Foulard said. "Them Indians are Comanche, Kane. That pony there has a Comanch' split ear."

Kane thumbed back the hammer of his carbine. "The pistol," he said with finality.

Foulard hesitated. Then he asked, "We're partners, ain't we, buddy?"

"I haven't made up my mind yet. Let's have the pistol."

Foulard silently gave it to him, butt first.

"Thanks," Kane said dryly.

They rode slowly upcanyon, letting the animals pick their own pace. The Indian pony was balky at first but settled down, perhaps reassured by the black gelding and mule. Kane spread out his troubled thoughts as he rode but he did not relax his vigilance. Foulard was an unknown quantity and this troubled him. He'd met men like Foulard before, usually men on the run drifting up and down the outlaw trail stretching between the territory on the south and the Brown's Hole hideout on the north, where the borders of Wyoming, Utah and Colorado touched. Foulard, Kane had determined, was cowardly, sly, shifty and yet capable of killing. Kane had no intention of letting Foulard get in a back shot, which was why, in spite of Foulard's protests, Kane brought up the rear.

Daylight found them out of the canyon. Kane turned north, urging the animals into a steady trot along a faint trace, probably an Indian trail, Kane thought, that followed a boulder-filled creek. Willows and cottonwoods grew along the bank but the land was bare except for scattered cactus and sage away from the stream.

In a clear grassy glade, screened by the trees, Kane stopped. The animals began grazing greedily even before being off-loaded and unsaddled. Kane started a fire with his burning glass, using dry wood that wouldn't make smoke. Foulard inspected the Indian pony. A blue jay scolded from an adjacent tree and a brown hawk darted down on a breakfast search.

They gulped a hasty meal of coffee and flapjacks, using the last bit of flour. Foulard looked critically at the Indian pony. "Comanch' all right," he declared. "Lookit that split ear. The Comanch' mark their horses like that."

Kane took the buckskin legging he had removed from

the dead Indian and tossed it at Foulard's feet. "I took this from one of them," he said.

Foulard's whiskery face looked pinched as he held up the footwear to examine it. "That's Apache," he muttered. "You hear me, Kane? That there's an Apache moccasin legging. Their squaws make 'em like that, a legging that comes up between their knee and thigh. In hot weather they roll 'em down and when they're runnin' through the brush they pull 'em up."

"You said Comanche."

"No. I said Comanch' pony. An' it is. That there's an Apache moccasin. Them Apache devils are bad medicine, Kane. Let's mosey on."

"Comanche pony, Apache boot."

Foulard looked all around apprehensively and then jumped to his feet, pointing. "See, what'd I tell you?"

Kane rose and looked in the direction Foulard pointed. Riders were coming through a defile into the valley. The distance was too great to tell if the riders were white or Indian. Kane looked at Foulard, who feverishly threw gear on the pack mule.

Foulard saw Kane's look. "Dammit, let's get outta here, man. Gonna stand there all day?"

Kane was looking in the other direction now, his eyes attracted by movement. He gestured, and Foulard, in the act of mounting the mule, stopped dead still. Three riders were sweeping in at a lope from the north.

"Giles!" Foulard exclaimed, turning to Kane, his mouth sagging. "That's Hugh Giles with his killer kid—and Zack Morton!"

Kane said, "Don't panic, Foulard. We'll keep to the brush and out of sight." He mounted and led out, keeping inside the brush on the creek side, hidden from both groups of approaching riders. Foulard's face was twisted with fear and he lashed at the mule with the ends of his reins and his heels drummed against the beast's sides.

The creek curved in here, toward the high buttes. Somewhere deep inside Kane felt a premonition, a warning signal from some unknown source but one he'd learned to heed. Hurried by Foulard's obvious fright, Kane pushed his horse through the thickening brush. He glimpsed the riders behind him as he twisted in the saddle, looking through the trees, seeing the rapid motion of the horses and riders.

Kane rode free of the trees and wheeled the black when he caught sight of Giles. The creek split here, one smaller branch murmuring out of a narrow canyon opening, the other meandering around the base of the red-brown butte.

"Let's hope this isn't a box canyon," Kane said, and put the uneasy black down into the water and splashed through to the opposite bank. They were effectively screened from the valley by the thick willows drooping over the creek, the leaves touching the unruly stream.

The black stumbled, snorted and regained his footing and went ahead between wind- and weather-sculptured stones rising high on either side, layered in browns, reds and yellows. There was a sudden thump of hoofbeats ahead and Kane drew his pistol, hauling the black in with his left hand. He half smiled, holstering his gun when a small band of wild horses wheeled away and clattered up the narrow canyon.

"Gawd, I thought it was them!" Foulard said hoarsely. "Gimmie that pistol again, Kane."

"Hold off," Kane said and stepped off the black and led him toward a bald rock rising from the water. He came along the edge of the creek where the wild horses had been drinking. Here, where he stood, he could see the length and breadth of the valley and yet was concealed from view of those riders galloping on a collision course yet unseen by each other. "It's not a blind canyon or those wild horses wouldn't have headed that way," Kane said.

Foulard, stinking of fear, splashed through the creek and dropped to the ground beside Kane. "You gonna lemme have that pistol?"

"No I'm not." Kane got his carbine from the saddle boot and laid it across the rim of boulder.

"What the hell you gonna do?"

"Can't let them ride into those Indians," Kane said. "Way they're heading now they'll run into them at that point coming out into the valley. They'll come on them sudden if we don't warn them somehow."

"You're crazy!" Foulard said loudly. "You don't know Giles or you wouldn't worry about what happens to him."

"He's a white man."

"His skin's white, yeah."

"Get that mule and the Indian pony further back into the rocks."

Foulard sullenly obeyed, leading the two animals back and tethering them by laying heavy stones on the reins. He came back and leaned against the rock beside Kane.

"You're gonna get us kilt."

"Not on purpose."

"Oh, hell, you're plain crazy," Foulard said in a hopeless voice. He leaned over and yanked the pistol out of Kane's holster and jammed it into Kane's side. His voice changed as he grated, "You ain't gonna get me kilt, you crazy sonofagun!"

Kane left the rifle where it lay across the rocks and turned slowly and looked at Foulard.

Spittle flew out of Foulard's mouth when he shouted,

"You don't know Giles like I do. He's a cold-blooded killer and nothin'—I mean nothin'—stops him."

"When it's your time to go you'll go."

"I ain't helpin' matters along. An' don't look at me like that!"

Kane said nothing, continuing to stare at Foulard.

"I'll pull this trigger so help me hannah!"

Kane smiled. "You emptied that gun last night, Foulard, shooting at Apaches. I never did reload it. You hurried me out of there before I could shuck out the empties and fill it up again."

Foulard's eyes glazed and his mouth opened. He looked stupidly at the gun in his hand.

Kane hit him a solid blow on the jaw and knocked him down. Kane leaned over and lifted the Colt from Foulard's hand and shoved it in his holster.

He ignored Foulard and turned to lean against the rock, cradling his carbine in his two hands. Giles and his riders were a hundred yards from him, sitting their horses, except for Zack Morton, who was on the ground beside his horse, apparently looking for a sign of their passing.

Off to the left, screened from Giles by a rocky point, the Indians came on at a gallop. Kane aimed his carbine, getting the leading rider in the buck-horn sight, following the motion of the Apache as well as he could.

Foulard groaned and sat up.

In that moment, Kane squeezed the trigger. The carbine fired, bucking against his shoulder. The brave on the lead pony disappeared over the rump of his pony. The others scattered, firing a ragged, disorganized volley. Kane glimpsed Giles and his men scuttling for cover, where they immediately opened fire.

The Apaches broke, scattering, some riding back the

way they'd come, others disappearing wraithlike into the rocks.

Giles and his men mounted hastily and gave chase. The sounds of firing subsided except for an occasional report that boomed lonesomely back and forth between the buttes.

Foulard sat on the ground watching Kane, rubbing his face. "You damn near broke my jawbone. You didn't have to do that."

"You didn't have to take my pistol."

Foulard pushed himself off the ground and got to his feet and looked at Kane. "Well, what're we gonna do now?"

Kane grinned as he reloaded his carbine. "Why don't we go get that gold? If it's there."

Foulard slapped his thigh. "Well now, that's more like what I wanted to hear."

Kane mounted the black, feeling relief that he'd not given in to his first urge to ride on without warning Giles. If he had given in to that compelling idea, he mused, it'd have been because of the gold. That treasure, if it existed, was beginning to assume an importance to him that he didn't particularly favor.

The gold could provide an answer to some of the problems that started when he was too young to understand what was happening.

Jared didn't know where he was born. His first memories were of Salt Lake City, the small red-brick house just off the Four Corners Road, where one of the bishops operated a general store. He didn't remember his mother, just the big, ample-breasted woman who "took care of the house" and Jared only incidentally. When John Kane married Christine Jared remembered his feeling of happiness on acquiring a mother, a real mother, who was pretty and smelled good.

His happiness lasted until more than a year after Preston, his stepbrother, was born.

Both his father and mother made it plain to Jared that he was responsible for Pres, as Preston was called, from the time the little boy learned to walk. The family moved out of Garnettville, to the ranch on Three Creek country, after Bishop Garnett was killed by the Indians.

Accepting his responsibility for Pres had not been too difficult until the younger brother reached his teens. He grew wilder and wilder and would accept no direction from either John or Christine. Pres went his own wild way until John Kane was lost in a stampede. After his father's death, Jared was made to feel that he was an outsider.

He remembered Preston's words very well, as though they'd happened yesterday. "This is the Garnett spread, Jared, and your name is Kane. Just remember that."

Not long after that Jared became a drifter. He felt better being away on his own, away from Pres and Christine.

CHAPTER 4

Kane looked on Armijo, drowsing in the sun below him, with something of disappointment. He didn't know what he'd expected but it certainly wasn't this: adobes, whitewashed a dazzling white, clustered in a loop of the creek, sheltered by quivering-leaved aspens, splashed with yellow. Beyond the narrow street of the village a larger adobe, almost as large as a hacienda, stood apart from the others. Smoke rose from a beehive oven, where women baked tortillas and children and goats played.

"You said it was deserted," Kane said through heat and wind-cracked lips. He'd not shaved since meeting Foulard and a two-week growth of his golden beard gleamed in the sun.

Foulard didn't answer, pointing wordlessly to the church, a stone building on the crest of a flat-topped butte, its cross outlined against the blue of the sky.

"There it is," Foulard exulted. "That's it, Kane, what we been lookin' for." He put the mule into motion, drumming his heels against the mule's gaunt ribcage.

"Wait up, Foulard."

"Wait? Man, I been waitin' all my born days. I ain't gonna wait no more, no more. Let's go." But he pulled the mule in, looking anxiously at Kane.

"People here," Kane said. "Look over there, Foulard." He pointed to a half-dozen canvas-covered wagons far up the creek, almost hidden by a grove of quaking aspen.

"People in the village here, too. The church doesn't appear to be abandoned like you said it would be."

"So what the hell. We didn't travel such a far piece to sit and look, did we?"

"You want to ride right up and start digging? Use your head, man."

Foulard shook his head as though to clear it. His eyes lost the glazed look, the crazy look. He blinked at Kane. "Well, what're we s'posed to do?"

"First thing is to check with the *alcalde* and get permission to camp here. And buy food. We're out of everything."

"I'm not gonna ast no damn greaser for nothin'."

"I'll do it."

Foulard shrugged resignedly. "Do what you hafta. It's up to you. But me, I wouldn't go beggin'—" He stopped speaking when he saw the look on Kane's face.

Kane put his horse in motion and rode among outcroppings of black lava rock, heading for the creek. He stopped the horse at the water's edge and dismounted and waited while the horse drank. Foulard followed, hauling on the Indian pony's lead rope. The mule and Indian pony joined the black and all the animals drank noisily.

Kane knelt above the animals, higher up the creek, and drank, savoring the cold water from the mountains higher above.

Afterward, they crossed the creek and went down the sloping grassy range and entered the village, making their way toward the largest adobe.

A scattering of pigs, goats and burros ignored them as they traversed the narrow, dusty street. The women could be seen at work between the adobe huts but paid them no mind except for shy side glances.

An old man sat in a bull-hide chair stationed in the

patio of the large adobe, screened from the wind by a low, weathered, brown adobe wall, a straw hat covering his face. The children, half-naked, played around the old man's feet, scrambled away with shrill cries of alarm and peering at them from the corner of the adobe wall.

The old man raised his straw hat from his wrinkled brown face. "*Buenos días, señores,*" he said, his bright, guileless brown eyes fastened on Kane. He was wrinkled as a sun-dried prune. "Dismount and rest your horses and your souls."

In his rusty, halting Spanish, Kane said, "Thank you, sir. May we have a drink of water?"

"Surely." He nodded and raised his voice: "Juanita!"

A slim girl with liquid brown eyes and jet-black hair in braids came shyly with a dripping gourd. The loose dress she wore reached to her ankles but did not conceal her lissome body. Foulard looked at her in open admiration.

Kane took the gourd from Juanita and drank. He passed the gourd to Foulard and said to the old man, "Thank you, sir. I've not had that kind of water in my lifetime."

"It is good when one comes from the desert." He looked at the gaunted gelding, the ladder-ribbed mule and the thin Indian pony. "You've traveled a great distance."

Kane nodded. "We would stay and rest our animals before moving on," he said. "If it meets with your approval."

"What're you sayin'?" Foulard asked.

Kane shook his head to silence Foulard.

"You may remain as long as you wish," the old man said, rising slowly, painfully. "My house is that of Gonzales. I am *jefe* of the village and I live in this house. My sons' wives and children live nearby and my daughter, Juanita, lives with me since she lost her husband." He looked at Kane. "And how are you called?"

"I am Kane. This is Foulard."

Gonzales offered a thin brown hand to each of them in turn. The children continued to stare at them from the security of the adobe wall.

"May we camp in the arroyo below the church?" Kane asked Gonzales.

Gonzales blinked. "You would be more comfortable in the grove by the creek."

"We may annoy your people and dirty the creek. I would rather camp in the arroyo if you don't mind."

Gonzales shrugged. "I don't mind at all. I was thinking of your comfort. You may camp where you will."

"The wagons toward the mountains," Kane said. "Are these some immigrants passing through?"

Gonzales shook his head, chuckling. "Crazy Americans —your pardon, sir—who look at the old Indian ruins and search for gold. They do not know there is no gold here. I told them so but they do not heed."

"He said somethin' about gold," Foulard broke in. "What'd he say, Kane, about gold?"

Kane frowned, shaking his head at Foulard again. "Have they been here long?" he asked Gonzales.

"Perhaps a fortnight," Gonzales said. "They are very rich, with fine horses and guns, and in this camp they live like kings—and queens."

"Queens? There are women among them?"

"Yes." Gonzales nodded, holding up two fingers.

"I thank you, sir," Kane said. "My friend thanks you."

Gonzales glanced at Foulard, looked back to Kane and nodded. "You are more than welcome," he said. "Is there anything I can do for you?"

"We need food," Kane said. "Yes, and feed for the animals."

Gonzales' withered face brightened. "Whatever you need, sir."

"Flour, bacon—"

"We have no flour, sir, but all the corn meal you may require."

"That is good. Thank you."

"My sons will bring what you need when you are camped." He extended his hand to Kane. "Come visit with an old man when you are settled in and have the time."

Kane nodded to Gonzales, winked at the children, who tittered and disappeared, and turned away, leading his horse. Foulard came after him, mouthing impatient questions when they were out of earshot.

"That ol' greaser said somethin' about gold. I understand that there word. What was it?"

"Those wagons camped up above, on the creek. Americans looking for gold."

"Not our gold?"

Kane laughed. "Our gold? It hasn't got our brand on it."

"It's mine—ours. They got no right—"

"We don't know who they are, why they're here. The old man, Gonzales, said they were looking at Indian ruins and mentioned gold in a joking way. Simmer down. Anyway, this may not be the place at all."

"This is the place!" Foulard insisted.

"I haven't seen the map yet."

"I'll show it to you soon's we make camp."

Kane stopped in the arroyo below the church. The stone building stood on a fifty-foot-high flat-topped mesa rising out of the benchland, overlooking the village and the valley. They always build in a place the people have to look up to, Kane thought. "The bell tower is new," Kane said, looking up at the dark stone outlined against a cloudless blue sky. "This is as good a place to camp as any."

"It's too fur from water."

"I'd rather carry water and be close where we can watch," Kane said. "We can't let anyone know what we're up to, Foulard. The villagers—or somebody—would stop us one way or another."

"Well, all right."

A black-robed priest appeared on the brink of the mesa over them and began descending a narrow path cut out of the black rock. He came into the arroyo and stopped.

"Good day, Father," Kane said. "We were admiring your church."

"Thank you." The priest smiled. He was a young man, with guileless brown eyes and a black beard. "It is sadly in need of repairs but we love it."

"It is very old, is it not?" Kane asked.

"What're you talkin' about?" Foulard asked.

The priest smiled at Foulard. "The church," he said in English.

"Hey, you speak Americano," Foulard said, pleased.

The priest nodded. "Yes. I attended an American university. The main building of our church is perhaps three hundred years old. The front portion is more recent, not more than a century."

Foulard whistled.

"I'm Father Caldero," the priest said and shook hands with both of them. "This sleepy little village of Armijo is so far removed from civilization. We seldom have visitors since the great tragedy."

"There's a camp up the creek," Kane observed.

"Ah, yes. A delightful party. A Spanish nobleman, an archaeologist from Boston, a doctor in anthropology—and a beautiful girl, the daughter of your Secretary of War."

"What's an arch—arch—them two things you said?" Foulard asked bluntly.

Father Caldero considered the question and then said, "An archaeologist is an uncoverer of the past. A digger in the dirt of history, one might say."

"An' that other thing?"

"Anthropologist. A student of the science of man."

"Ummm." Foulard cleared his throat. "I see."

"We'd like to camp here," Kane said. "We'll pasture our animals in that little valley over there." He gestured. "We'll need a little time to recover from the desert."

The priest nodded. "Welcome to Armijo," he said, and nodding, moved along the path toward the village.

"Father," called Kane, and the priest stopped, turned and tilted his head to a listening position. His dark face, shadowed by a wide-brimmed, round-crowned black hat, was open and friendly as he waited.

"This tragedy you mentioned?"

Father Caldero's smile disappeared. "Ah, yes. You may have noticed we have no men here, other than Jesus Gonzales, the chief, and his two sons. All the other males were killed by the Apache two years ago in an uprising of violence and bloodshed." He made a sign of the cross.

"All of them?" Kane asked and Father Caldero nodded. Kane went on, "That's terrible. I'm sorry, Father."

"Nantana spared the women and children so they could warn others."

Father Caldero bowed his head a moment and then looked at Kane. "It was God's will," he said, and walked on.

"Good godfrey," Foulard muttered. "A whole town full of women and no men." He licked his lips.

"We came here for gold," Kane said.

Foulard grinned. "An' anythin' else that drops inter our hands," he said.

Kane stepped close to Foulard and grasped the man's

shirt, suddenly angry. "Forget about the women of Armijo, Foulard," he said between clenched teeth, "or by God, I'll wring your damn worthless neck."

"Good lordy," Foulard said. "Ain't no call to bite my head off. Lemme go, now. I ain't aimin' t' bother nobody." He hastily stepped back as Kane released him.

"Damn," he muttered under his breath. "Ain't never seen you git mad afore."

"Just stay away from the village," Kane said and hoped that Foulard would do just that.

But he wasn't fully convinced.

CHAPTER 5

Hugh Giles rode in silence with his son, Bud, and Zack Morton, the horses walking in the intense heat of the sun. He'd grown eager as the trail they followed freshened but as his eagerness grew his caution increased.

"Ought to be catching up tomorrow or the next day," Giles said. "We can't be far behind them now."

No one bothered to answer. It was too hot to talk.

Since taking the trail with Zack and Bud, Hugh Giles's anticipation had grown in direct proportion to the distance traveled. He was like a keenly tuned hunting animal, alert, pressing on, yet conserving his horse and himself. This was an old story to him. He was good at it and he knew he was good.

And to make the cheese more binding, he thought, there's a hell of a lot at stake.

The trail he followed grew dim and indistinct. Zack Morton said, "I better get down and take a look."

The horses were only too happy to stop. Zack Morton dismounted and grounded his reins and went ahead, scanning the ground. He retraced his steps and knelt in the sand beside his horse, puzzled at the sign. "Well, it looks—" He raised startled eyes at Hugh Giles's sudden shout. A single gunshot racketed through the hot silence as a group of hard-riding horsemen broke from behind a ridge of rock ahead. The lead rider tumbled over the rump of his horse. The others wheeled up short.

Giles counted five Indians mounted and one on the ground, then he was on the ground firing at the next horseman, levering another shell into his Winchester and looking for another target in the milling mass of riders and horses.

The Indians wheeled and circled uncertainly and then reversed as though on command, going back in the direction from which they'd come.

Giles ran to his horse. "Don't let 'em get away," he shouted. "We'll have 'em on our ass from here on out if we don't get 'em all now!"

Zack and Bud followed Giles and rapidly closed the distance between them and the retreating Apache. As they entered the arroyo from which the Apache came, a new group exploded from a shallow canyon on the right, firing as they came. Another small bunch broke from cover on the left. The small band they'd pursued now turned back.

Hugh Giles watched Zack and Bud go down and he heard his horse scream as it staggered. He disengaged his feet from the stirrups as a club-swinging brave came from behind. Hugh Giles and the horse went down together. Giles lay on the ground, unable to move but hazily aware of what was happening to his two companions.

Two braves stripped Zack Morton of his guns and clothing. One of the braves put on Zack's sombrero and did a shuffle around the dead man. Another buckled Zack's gunbelt around his waist, unsheathing the gun and firing it into the air. Still another Indian put on Zack's leather vest and strutted back and forth.

Hugh sat up as a tall Apache motioned with his hands and the Indians fell on Zack's body with their knives, cutting off his privates and slicing open the thighs. The Apache did not go near Bud Giles.

A word from the leader and Hugh Giles was dragged before the tall man, towering above his short, stocky braves.

"I am Nantana," he said proudly, his muscular arms crossed over his deep chest. His face was classic, with a fiercely curved nose and an imperious tilt of his head. He uncrossed his arms and fingered a blue and gold medallion that hung from his neck. He spent some time telling Giles what a great warrior he was and how he meant to kill off all the white-eyes who wouldn't leave his country. "This is my land," he said. "The white-eyed general called Crook is preparing to make war on my people. Tell me, how many soldiers does he have? What are his plans, white man?"

"That's out of my line," Hugh Giles said. "I don't even know a general named Crook."

A brave hit him across the head with a war club and knocked him over. He struggled up, but did not stand. He was sitting in the sand, dazed, thinking this red sonofabitch is going to kill me if I don't give him some answers. Maybe he'll kill me anyway but I gotta try something. He raised his head and looked at Nantana, trying to remember some of the gossip he'd heard about the army. Some bits and pieces came to his mind. "General Crook is going to train his soldiers to fight Indians before he takes up the warpath. That's about all I know, Nantana."

Nantana looked at him with a sharp penetrating gaze. He spoke in Apache and two of the braves began cutting chunks of meat from Giles's dead horse. The meat was placed in buckskin sacks. The band mounted up. Giles thought for a moment they'd leave him there. But Bud Giles's horse was brought near and Nantana, with a sardonic smile on his face, motioned for Giles to mount.

The band rode out with Giles in the middle of a tight little circle of Apache warriors.

Giles avoided looking at his dead son's body beyond Morton's mutilated form.

CHAPTER 6

At sundown Kane and Foulard had finished their chores. The camp was as comfortable as was possible in the dry arroyo below the church. A frame of poles held Kane's tarp, making a shelter of sorts. The girl, Juanita, accompanied by two squat, sullen men, brought supplies.

Now by a small fire, drinking coffee from tin cups, Kane said, "The new part of the church covers the stairway to the underground chamber, if your map is right."

"It's right."

"We'll find out. Now suppose we tunnel in from that spot beside the rock." He pointed with his cup.

"It'd be quicker to dig right down inside the church."

"We can't do it that way. No way. We're going to have to do it quietly so no one will know what we're up to."

"We start diggin' inside the church and we'd be through in one night. We'll get it and get out." Foulard sounded more stubborn than usual.

"If anything happened and we couldn't get through in one night we'd give it away," Kane said patiently. "It'll take longer to go in from outside but it's our best bet. We can dump the dirt we dig out in that crevice there. We'll work at night."

"Got it all figgered, ain't y'?" Foulard said. He gave his head a twitch. "God! Just think—twenty feet through that dirt there."

Kane rose, tossing the dregs in his cup away. "I'm going

to get cleaned up and drop by that camp up the creek," he said. "While I'm talking to them you slip into that ruin up there where they've been working and steal a pick and shovel."

"A pick 'n' shovel?"

Kane nodded. "We need them to dig with, Foulard. That's two pieces of equipment I never thought I'd need so I didn't bring them."

"All right, I'll do it."

"Don't leave camp until full dark," Kane said. "And don't let anyone see you prowling around."

"You must think I'm stupid," Foulard growled.

Kane didn't answer but headed for the creek with soap, shaving gear and clean clothing. Smoke from cooking fires blended with the dusk of evening. A few stars were out in the darkening sky.

Kane walked along the edge of the adobe town, smelling the spicy odor of cooking chilies, aware that as a stranger he was attracting attention. Not openly. Many eyes watched from slitted windows.

A fringe of cottonwoods and willows lined both banks of the creek. Kane turned off the trail and went among the trees, tramping upstream until he found a deep pool formed by an elbow turn on the creek.

In a grassy glade enclosed by brush he shed his clothing and waded out to swim. The water was chill, fresh from the mountains. He washed away all traces of the desert through which he had passed.

When he was clean he swam until he tired, then drifted to a finger of sand and scrubbed again with soap and sand. He rinsed off, swam back across the pool. He climbed out and stood on the bank and shook himself dry. He dressed in clean underwear, shirt and trousers. He stood in the water, rinsing first one foot and then the other before stepping to a clean spot where he pulled on clean socks and stamped his feet back into his boots.

Fully dressed, he squatted beside the stream and began shaving, hurriedly, for dark was falling fast.

Hearing a twig snap, he raised quickly, leaning toward the bush where he'd draped his gunbelt. He lifted his pistol from the holster and, with the gun ready, parted the brush. A dark-haired woman was undressing on the bank of the stream. She was slipping a dress over her head and he glimpsed her firm, well-rounded body.

"Wait a moment," he called and heard the swift intake of her breath.

She clutched the dress to her body, staring at him. She was a strikingly attractive woman, dark hair pinned up, with large eyes whose color he couldn't tell, and a full, curved mouth.

"What—what're you doing here?"

"Same thing you are," he said. "Just stay where you are until I get the rest of my whiskers off and then I'll go."

He followed her eyes and looked down to see he was still holding the pistol. He shoved it in his belt and went to finish shaving.

"Don't hurry," the woman called. "After all, you were here first."

"Nearly finished," Kane said. "Didn't expect to find anyone around. Especially a—a white woman." He nicked himself with the razor and muttered a curse.

"I'm with a group of people from the East and from Europe," she said.

"None of my business but this is Apache country."

"It's close to a settlement."

"A village that lost all their menfolk two years ago."

"That was two years ago."

"My partner and I killed three Indians on the warpath not far from here just a few days ago."

He heard her intake of breath again. "Killed them! You —you sound bloodthirsty!"

"Not at all. They were trying to kill us." He scraped the last patch of whiskers away, rinsed his face with creek water and put his shaving gear away. "Well, that's that. So long, ma'am."

"Wait," she commanded. "Stay out of sight until I finish. Perhaps you should escort me back to camp. It's nearly dark."

"Perhaps I should," he said good-naturedly and stowed his gear on the grass and sat down. It was a still time of day, with the sudden western night coming down fast, placing a lonely beauty on the land. He listened to the plaintive call of a dove, and the woman splashing in the creek. He visualized her in all the loveliness he'd barely glimpsed. A lady, this one, if he was any judge.

She parted the brush and stepped through and he got to his feet. She seemed taller but it may have been the luxuriant growth of dark hair piled high on her head. Her face had a clean, scrubbed look. She held out her hand and said, "It was nice of you to wait. I'm Maurine Summers."

He took her extended hand. "Jared Kane. You're General Summers' daughter?"

She laughed, nodding in a pleased way. "I'm surprised you know the name. Not many Westerners know the Secretary of War."

He chuckled. "Father Caldero told me."

"Oh, you've met him?"

He nodded and stepped back and she went ahead of him to the faint trail that led off upstream.

She turned her head, looking at him, slowing until he came abreast of her. "At least you're—"

He moved close, placed his hand over her mouth, holding her with his other arm.

She stiffened in his arms and then relaxed.

Not a dozen feet away an Apache warrior, crouched in the brush, was looking at the camp upriver. He carried a rifle in both hands.

The Apache rose slowly and walked forward another dozen feet and disappeared into the shadows without a sound.

Maurine moved and he tightened his hold on her. They waited, holding their breath, Kane listening to the night sounds.

After a long wait, Kane relaxed his hold on her. "He's gone," he said.

"What—what was he doing here?" Her voice was a whisper.

"Scouting your camp."

"But—but I didn't think Indians moved around at night."

"Maybe not in the old days. But many of these Apache have scouted for the Army, have picked up a lot of the white man's ways." He could smell the odor of the soap she'd used recently. "An Apache would brave more than the dark for a young woman."

"I'm not afraid."

"There are times when it pays to be afraid."

"How did you come to be here?"

The night had come down solid but the gleam of fires above guided them. Once she stumbled and he caught her arm, feeling the firm, warm flesh beneath his fingers.

"You didn't answer me," she said.

"Why do I have to tell you how I come to be here?"

"All right. I won't pry. I've heard that it's not proper to be too inquisitive out here."

"Why are you here?" he asked.

"Your tone says something else. Like perhaps I don't belong here."

"There might be some truth in what you say."

"We have a squad of cavalry from Fort Defiance. And a civilian scout, too. We came well prepared. One of the men, a Spanish nobleman, Prince Luis Cabeza Narbona, fought in the Spanish Army and has been decorated for bravery."

"I hope no Apache hears of him. They hate Spaniards with a passion."

"For goodness sake, why?"

"The Spanish deceived, robbed and raped them for several hundred years."

"And built missions, educated them, taught them how to live."

Kane laughed shortly. "All a matter of viewpoint."

They left the creek and slowly walked into the circle of light. Several people rose from camp chairs and stared at Kane.

Kane took in the camp with one sweeping glance.

The man who walked to meet them was of medium height. A slim and handsome man in a white dinner jacket, with jet-black hair and dark brown eyes, polished boots and a stiff formal manner. His white shirt had ruffles at the front and wrists and was crisply clean.

"Mr. Kane, Prince Luis Cabeza Narbona of Madrid . . ."

The prince clicked his heels, bowing from the waist, and didn't offer his hand. "Thank you for escorting Miss Summers back to camp, Kane."

Actually, Kane observed three camps; the main one,

made by two wagons placed together at right angles and covered with a huge canvas, held a white cloth-covered table, gleaming crystal ware and silver sparkling light from fire reflection. Off to one side still another wagon, another campfire, around which squatted cavalrymen of the U. S. Army. Still another fire and a third camp held teamsters and civilian employees. Near a complete field kitchen, Kane watched a chef in a tall white hat preparing food. Kane had never seen such a group before and suppressed a desire to laugh at the ridiculousness of it all.

Maurine Summers walked farther into the circle and introduced the others: Dr. Porter Canfield, a tall, elegant, slender man with slightly stooped shoulders and the absent-minded air of a traditional college professor. Canfield's wife, blond with a doll-like prettiness spoiled by sharp features, gave Kane an arch smile. Dr. Sean Flannery, of Boston, and no black Irish this one, but a ruddy-faced intellectual. From the glass in his hand and his veined face, Kane judged him to be addicted to strong drink. All of them were casually curious but evidenced no excitement, even when Maurine mentioned their sighting an Apache.

"Probably that surly fellow from the village," Prince Narbona remarked.

"You people would be wise to circle up your wagons," Kane said. "The Apache are out in force."

Narbona's dark eyes glittered. "I'd welcome a chance at them. It's my hope that I will not return to Spain without the opportunity to meet with them. One in particular."

"More than a hundred years ago, the Apache attacked Taos in great numbers, killed the men and kidnaped many women, Luis' maternal great-grandmother among them," Maurine explained.

"That must have been in 1760," Kane said, "at Vidal-pando house."

Prince Luis' dark eyebrows lifted. "It was indeed," he said, looking at Kane with new interest.

There was a scuffling sound outside the camp, and Foulard staggered into the firelight pushed by a tall, mus-tached man wearing a fancy Mexican jacket and chaps.

"Jake! What is this?" Maurine asked.

"This fellow was skulking around the ruins where you were working today," Jake said, putting his keen black eyes on Kane.

"This is Jake Lugo, our scout," Maurine said.

"I wasn't doin' nothin'," Foulard whined. "I was jes'—"

"This man is with me," Kane said. "He's my partner."

All of them looked from Foulard to Kane.

"He's all right," Kane insisted. "Probably just curious."

Another man moved out of the night and into the firelight. Kane looked again at an officer of the U. S. Army in full dress uniform.

As the officer stopped and bowed, Maurine introduced him as Lieutenant Henry Jay, commanding the military escort from Fort Defiance. The officer was little more than a cherubic-faced boy with deep-blue eyes, red cheeks and blond hair, very correct and formal. He touched his hat with a gloved hand, bringing it away with a snap that brought a faint smile to Kane's lips.

"Did I hear you say something about Apache?" he asked Kane.

"My partner and I had a brush with them several days ago," Kane said. "Three of them tried to ambush us. Then several days later, another bunch attacked a white party who were not with us."

"That's right," Foulard said eagerly. "Me 'n' Kane here killed three of them buggers."

"Strange," said Lieutenant Jay, shaking his head. "My scout says they're quiet."

"I haven't seen any sign," Jake Lugo said.

"My understanding is that the Apache are all safely on reservations," Jay said, his youthful face troubled.

"Join us for cocktails and dinner," Prince Luis said, changing the subject, without cordiality.

"Thank you, no," Kane said. "Your camp is a prime target for the Apache. There's everything here they want—horses, mules, women, guns, liquor—and they'll probably try to take it."

"Maybe the Apache don't know we're here," Jay said.

"They know. They know everything that goes on in *their* country. I'd post a guard and circle the wagons if I were you." Kane looked around the circle of faces. "Good night," he said, touching his hand to his hat. "Let's go, Foulard."

Walking through the darkness, Foulard said, "Good God almighty, Kane. We got ourself in a hornet's nest. You think them Apache gonna hit us?"

"I was trying to scare that party out of here," Kane said. "It'll be easier for us if they're not here."

"Whew!" Foulard sighed. "You really had me scairt."

"You better stay scared," Kane said. "I'm just guessing. But we've seen more Apache on the warpath than for a long, long time. They may be up to something."

High on the slope above the Summers' camp, a lone Apache hidden in the rock crevices above the ruins watched the merrymaking, the drinking and eating, waited patiently until all the fires died. He waited until total darkness cloaked the area. Then he came to his feet, slipped noiselessly to his pony and swung up, heading for Nantana's rancheria. His unshod pony made small sounds that carried only a few feet.

He didn't know it but his precautions were not necessary. No guards were posted around the camp.

Prince Luis Narbona had laughed away Lieutenant Henry Jay's fears as groundless.

CHAPTER 7

Hugh Giles realized that something big was in the wind as Nantana led his band north like a horde of scavengers. He rode in the middle of the growing band, his hands tied to the horn of his saddle, surrounded by Nantana's warriors.

On the march like a violent, unpredictable whirlwind, Nantana paused to stalk a wagon train. Giles was guarded by a single, sulking brave, as the others swooped in on the train, killed the muleskinners and ransacked the loaded wagons, looking for guns and bullets.

Nantana, blood on his hands from a fresh scalp, gave Giles a triumphant look and drew a thumb across his jaw. "This is how we do it," he said, and led the band onward, riding close-packed with a couple of scouts ranging ahead.

This jasper knows how to make war, Giles thought with feelings of fear he hadn't experienced in years. Nantana had something in mind for him or he wouldn't be taking the trouble with him that he had. Giles could only guess at his fate.

At nightfall, Nantana brought his warriors to a halt in a cottonwood grove beside a thin trickle of water. Giles was staked out at once, spread-eagled on the ground, gathering thrusts from a lance, a head-shaking blow from a war club. He lay quietly, naked except for his pants. Nantana's warriors had confiscated everything else he owned.

He managed to keep from shivering from the sudden drop in temperature as the sun went down.

Nantana squatted near a small fire, gnawing on a piece of half-raw horse meat. He looked across the fire at Giles and tossed the piece of meat he was gnawing on. It landed on Giles's chest, bounced, and Giles caught it in midair between his teeth.

The Apache looked at this with interest, laughing and pointing. Giles hated himself but he gnawed and sucked on the meat, careful not to let it fall from his mouth. He'd not eaten since being captured and he didn't know how long that had been. He'd lost all sense of passing hours or days.

In the stillness just before dawn, Giles was loosened and prodded with lances into the saddle where his hands were again tied to the saddle horn. After a short ride, the Apache band drew up on a flat-topped mesa overlooking a circular valley. A prosperous-appearing ranch lay in the center of the valley, seemingly with the inhabitants still sleeping. Nothing moved around the large, sprawling house surrounded by a cluster of barns, sheds and corrals. From the bits of talk he managed to pick up, Giles concluded Nantana was after horses, for which the ranch was famed. Nantana waved his braves into action and they quickly spread out on a line, not in a rush as Giles remembered them attacking the wagon train, but in a slow canter. He watched with a rising sense of being the only spectator to a massacre sure to follow.

He watched the progress of the riders, unwillingly admiring their horsemanship, though he knew them to be equally at home on foot, running through brush and cactus with the agility of deer. In that split second, as if on signal, the horses were in a hard-driving gallop, just as the sky flushed pink, outlining the mountains to the east. He heard the first shot seconds after seeing the bloom of black smoke, belching from the ranch. That shot had no effect on the headlong rush of the Apache horsemen. The Indians began to bark and whoop, their cries coming faintly to Giles. The brave guarding him looked at him with hate in his black eyes.

A man ran out from the nearest small shed and went down before a thrown lance. Nantana's horse leaped over the fallen man. The Apache circled while three of the warriors opened the large corral gate where restless horses surged around the circular corral.

It was all over almost before Giles could understand what was happening. The band of horses, loosely herded, came thundering down on him and his own horse was in motion as several braves dropped back to cover the retreat, firing on the ranch.

The knot of loose horses raised a cloud of dust and Giles's guard moved in closer, lashing his horse into a harder run to keep up.

Nantana appeared out of the dust and ran his horse beside Giles. Giles muttered a curse. The tall Apache leader had a bundle slung across his mount's withers and screams came from the bundle and rounded legs kicked in the air. Her hair flying in the wind, her nightgown flapping, the woman continued to scream until Nantana forced her head against the sweaty hide of his horse.

The band swept onward. Giles's horse, under control of the guard, headed off as the brave herded straying horses back to the main herd. Giles breathed the dust of the captured horses, now and then catching a glimpse of Nantana with his captive, now still, probably unconscious, Giles speculated.

Nantana led his braves to one of the water seeps known only to the Apache so the animals could drink. The stop gave Giles his first good look at Nantana's captive.

Nantana let her slip to the ground and then dismounted with a bound and proudly turned her around and around so that all could see his prize. She shook with fear, her face a white mask matching the thin nightgown she wore. The burnoose tumbled down revealing a golden, shining sheen of thick hair and she looked up, directly at Giles, her face brightening with hope that dulled as she saw his bound hands.

Giles looked away, not meeting her eyes.

One of the blooded captive horses had been hit by a stray bullet. At Nantana's orders a brave slit the animal's throat, and after a brief interval, with blood spouting, the horse sank to its knees and then flattened to the ground. The braves hurriedly cut out chunks of meat to store in their buckskin sacks.

Giles, watching the girl secretively, discerned from her drooped, quivering shoulders that she mourned the death of the horse, perhaps one of her own.

Giles continued to watch her surreptitiously as they proceeded toward some point north and east. He had not felt pity for a long time and he found the feeling strange and unsettling.

The band continued to grow larger as they traveled. Yet Giles had not seen one brave join the party. They must, he thought, join singly or in pairs but never once did he detect any new member joining the party. He saw new faces, not knowing where they came from. Nantana was gathering recruits and Giles could guess that the tall Apache was preparing for all-out war. What the hell does it matter to me? he thought sourly. My own ass is in a sling and I better be thinking about that.

Two days north of Pinos Altos, where the ranch had

been attacked, the band of braves turned into a rocky, stark and bare canyon, with high ragged walls twisting crookedly upward.

Giles could smell water and the animal he rode could sense its nearness too.

Turning into an offshoot canyon, midway up the mountain, they came at last to the *rancheria*, a spacious, grassed valley enclosed with high walls. A dozen wickiups and hide shelters scattered along a stream and ponies grazed on the lush valley grass. Smoke rose from many cooking pots. From the creek up to the base of the enclosing cliffs, a distance of nearly a half mile, century plants grew in profusion as though cultivated. The Apache depended on it for many things—food, drink and even needle and thread.

Amid yells and shrill screams, the Apache braves, women and children descended on the war party.

Nantana leaped off his pony and stood tall and haughty, his arms folded over his massive chest, a picture of pride in conquest and victory. He unfolded his arms slowly and raised them over his head and began speaking of the adventures of he and his warriors. Wisely, he didn't mention the braves lost.

"We will go back to the old ways," he promised.

He left off his speech-making and pointed to Giles. Two braves approached, put a rawhide cord around his neck and staked him out. One of them built a small, slow fire close to his head. The Apache, all of them men, women and children, crowded in and watched intensely.

Giles strained against his bonds and tried to push his head toward the fire. This is what they have been waiting for, he thought, as he succeeded in getting close enough to the fire for his hair to flame up. The watching horde watched curiously, without emotion.

Then, at another word from Nantana, a brave pushed

the fire away with his moccasined foot. Nantana squatted
before him, staring at him in silence, and then rose, spew-
ing out a rapid stream of Apache. The crowd melted
away.

Someone began a slow heavy beat on the drum. Cooking fires were replenished. Clearly, this was a day for
feasting and celebration.

The Apache were eating mutton and mule meat, their
faces shiny with the grease of animal fat. Nantana stood
before his wickiup, looking at his people with pride.
Where he led they would follow, now that he'd brought
good fortune to his ragtag following from a half-dozen
different tribes.

Hi-ya, he thought, and a deep feeling, as big as the sky,
filled him. He had led his band into the white man's do-
main and with the cost of only a few braves. It was now
time for the dance. He stuck his head into his wickiup and
ordered his wife out. She was his second wife, a Mexican
woman captured five years before in a raid into Mexico.
She had not borne him children and she aged quickly living with Nantana.

Nantana signaled and the lone drum was joined by
others. The braves left off their feeding and began circling the large fire to the beat of the drums.

When Nantana joined the other dancers around the
fire, all of his braves withdrew in a circle, watching in fas-
cination as Nantana danced alone, holding a stick in his
hand. He circled the fire four times and then stopped before a drummer who ceased his beat, waiting. Nantana
struck the drum a mighty blow and threw the stick into
the air so that it would fall among a group of braves. The
warriors dodged away as the stick came down. If the stick
hit them they'd take Nantana's wife. None wanted her because she bled all the time.

"There goes my wife. I throw her away!" Nantana shouted.

Watching all this, Giles thought, that red sonofabitch has traveled some; that's a Cheyenne doodad.

Nantana approached the young Mexican girl he'd captured and untied her and led her toward his wickiup.

"Do you also eat bear meat as the Cheyenne do?" Giles asked mockingly.

Nantana stopped abruptly. He stood there facing away from Giles for a long moment while the hushed crowd watched. Nantana turned slowly and stared at Giles. He nodded to the Mexican woman he'd just cast off and handed the young girl to her and spoke softly. With that he turned and swiftly went up the slope toward the place where he talked to his spirits.

Giles cursed silently. He had enough trouble of his own without asking for more. He couldn't forget the piercing look of pure hatred Nantana had put on him before he went silently away.

Jared Kane stood outside the canvas shelter he had erected as protection against the sun and wind. He stood there looking at the adobes of Armijo, pinkish somehow in the morning sun, with red peppers hanging in strings against the walls. Pigs and chickens nosed and scratched in the dusty ground around the adobes.

Behind him, Foulard crawled out into the open and stood up, yawning, stretching and scratching. "When we gonna start diggin'?"

"When we get tools," Kane said shortly. "You messed up last night, Foulard. Remember?"

"Aw, shoot, I didn't do nothin'."

"You sure as hell didn't. I need a little more time to look things over, anyway. We've got to be careful."

"We got to be careful way out here in the middle o' nowhere?"

"The Apache are out and hunting. We've got that bunch from back East. And there's Gonzales and the villagers. Maybe it is the middle of nowhere but let's do it my way."

Foulard grunted.

"You want to run the show?" Kane asked, struggling with his irritation.

"Well, no, I reckon not." Foulard grinned suddenly and Kane followed his sudden look of interest. Juanita stood in the doorway of her father's hacienda, shading her eyes from the sun with her hand. Even at a distance her sensuous curves were evident and Kane found himself responding to the sight. She dropped her hand as she saw them watching her, turning back into the hacienda.

"Don't go near the village," Kane said, and walked across the arroyo to the path leading up to the top of the mesa where the church stood.

"You treat me like a snot-nosed kid," Foulard said. "In case you wanna know, I wasn't aimin' to go down there."

Kane didn't respond but climbed the steep path to the top of the mesa and stood looking at the church. It was quiet there, and the sun, warm and golden, lent a soft patina to the old stone of the building. A corner of the church had fallen in, the stones scattered about. An air of neglect and decay hung over the primitive structure.

Father Caldero padded out from around the corner of the church and stopped at the sight of Kane. Smiling, he said, "Good morning, sir. I must apologize for my poor church."

"It's a shame for it all to fall in that way," Kane said. "Look, my father was a stonemason. He taught me a thing or two about laying stone. I'll gladly repair that corner. At least it'll stop further damage."

"We have no money to pay for such services," Father Caldero said, still smiling. The skin above his black beard under his eyes glowed with health, bronze-red.

"I meant to donate my services."

"You're of the faith?"

"I have no church," Kane said stiffly. "I grew up among people of the Mormon following."

The priest nodded. "It would make me happy to see something done for our church. Since all the men of Armijo—well, there is little the women can do."

"How do they live? The women?"

Father Caldero put out his hands, palms up. "Poorly. The grow vegetables and corn and have fruit trees and vineyards. But the irrigation ditches are in bad condition. The water does not flow well to the village gardens."

"They live from their gardens?"

The priest nodded. "Yes. There is an itinerant peddler who comes here now and then. On his travels this Jew collects money and other things for the widows and children. His coming is a highlight in the lives of the villagers."

"The camp upstream. They seem to be very rich people. Did they offer to help?"

"Only Prince Luis and the Boston professor are Catholic. They have made generous offerings to our church. Both are good men, though Professor Flannery drinks excessively."

"They live very well for such rough surroundings."

"Indeed they do." The priest stared at Kane, looking him straight in the eye. "What is troubling you, my son?"

Kane smiled. The man calling him *my son* was likely younger. "You think I'm troubled?"

"Most men carry burdens of one kind or another. It appears in many forms. You have a sadness . . ."

Kane felt the familiar constriction in his chest, and again, for the thousandth time, relived that day . . .

Jared had been instructed by Christine to put an end to the cattle thieving going on. Jared ran into a small group of rustlers putting a new brand on Garnett cattle. In the shoot-out, Pres was killed. He'd been a member of the group of thieves, for some unknown reason, stealing his own cows. Jared did not know he was shooting at his stepbrother until the young man lay dying on the ground. . . .

"I killed my brother," Kane said.

"And why do you flee?"

Kane smiled briefly, without humor. "You think I'm running?"

Father Caldero nodded.

"I guess you're right. He was my half brother. We had the same father. Mormons make no distinction in such matters."

"We're all brothers."

"Maybe."

Father Caldero clucked softly. "I fear for you, my friend."

Kane shrugged. "I ran because there would have been trouble. I didn't want to shoot anyone, ever again."

"That's a worthy resolve. God will bless you for it." He stared at Kane again. "You want to repair our church in penance?"

Kane shook his head. "No. That is not the reason."

"Penance is not a bad thing."

"What happened couldn't be avoided."

"I understand." Father Caldero was silent for a long stretching moment. "I accept your offer of help with gratitude. I can offer you nothing to aid you in doing this work."

"That's all right. I can likely get anything I may need from the rich people." He nodded in the direction of Maurine Summers' camp.

"Good," Father Caldero said and turned his steps toward the village. He hesitated, stopped and then swung around and returned to stand before Kane.

"There are old legends about buried treasure in this region," he said.

"So I've heard," Kane said, not betraying the sudden hurried beat of his heart.

"The stories are many. Some of them tell of gold buried by the Spanish fathers centuries ago. None of the stories are true." He turned away and continued toward the village.

Kane followed slowly, down the steep path to the camp.

"What'd he say?" Foulard asked.

"He says there's no gold around here, that it's all a fake story, tall tales."

"That ain't so!" Foulard cried in anguish. "Ol' Pete wouldn't lie to me, not on his deathbed, would he?"

"I didn't know old Pete."

"Don't believe that holy roller, Kane. He's jus' tryin' to get us to move on."

"That's possible," Kane admitted. "This is a very poor church. If there were gold and he knew of it he could change things in this valley." He stared down at the village, where Father Caldero had reached the house of Gonzales. The priest turned into the patio, crossed it and without knocking entered the adobe.

Why, Kane wondered, had Father Caldero volunteered the information that no treasure was to be found here?

How would he know they were remotely interested in gold? Did the priest have some inner knowledge not known to ordinary men, knowledge that permitted him to look into another's mind?

Kane chuckled at the thought.

"It ain't nothin' to laugh at," Foulard muttered.

"Was I laughing? I didn't know it, Foulard. Look, you stay close to camp. I'm going to walk up the creek and ask people to loan us tools."

"You gonna ast? You'll give it away."

"No, I'll tell them it's to repair the church. From what Father Caldero has told me they'll let us have what we need. Without questions."

"Well, if you say so," Foulard said doubtfully, and sat down on a boulder and watched Kane walk toward the camp up the creek.

CHAPTER 8

Kane tossed the shovel, pick and bag of small tools he'd borrowed from the Summers' party to the ground beside the corner of the church. He removed his shirt, revealing a pad of golden hair on his chest. The sun felt good on his body as he cleaned the caked sand and lime from the stone he planned to reuse in building up the corner that had fallen in due to wind, weather and settling of the earth.

He stacked the fallen stone in a neat pile and removed more large loose stones from the foundation.

It was good to feel the firm, rough surface of the stone in his hands. He remembered helping his father lay the stones for the Mormon church in Garnett.

Foulard appeared over the edge of the mesa and flung himself on the ground, watching Kane silently. Finally, he said, "You got a pick an' shovel, I see."

"Everything we need."

"We gonna dig right straight down to the gold through that hole in the corner?"

Kane wiped sweat from his forehead with the back of his hand. "That wouldn't be smart, would it?"

"You mean you're slavin' away here for nothin'?"

"No. We've got to do some planning. I've told you before we can't work openly. We can use our time to figure out just how to go about getting the gold—if it's there."

"Workin' for nothin' is not to my likin'."

"It won't be for nothing if we can do what we want without getting people excited."

"What I say is get it and get out fast. We'll be gone before they know—" He broke off as first one man and then another appeared over the rim of the mesa. The sons of Gonzales, Ramon and Felipe, dark, squat and ugly, came to stand in silence, staring abashedly at Kane.

"Good days, sirs," Kane said.

Ramon, the older one, nodded. "Our father sent us."

"He would have us assist you in repair of the church," Felipe added.

"Fine," said Kane. "We'll need sand from the creek, with no rocks, even small ones, in the sand."

"We'll get baskets from the village," Ramon said, "in which to carry the sand."

"What're they yappin' about?" Foulard growled.

"They want to help," Kane said to Foulard.

"I'd say they wanna spy on us," Foulard muttered.

Kane spoke to the brothers: "And lime. We need lime, and of course water to mix the lime and sand."

"The baskets woven by our women will also carry water, sir," Ramon said.

The two of them went away. Kane got a chipping hammer and trowel from the sack provided by one of the employees of the Summers' party. He began cleaning old residue from the stone, chipping away with the hammer while Foulard watched unhappily.

Working away, Kane glanced curiously at Foulard. The hardships of the trail barely showed now, but Foulard would always, even at his best, look as though he'd been pulled through a knothole.

"I been thinkin', Kane," said Foulard, scratching his armpit. "Maybe it's all too much. Say we dig a hole fifty feet through that malpais, under the church, an' then there ain't nothin' there."

"That's a chance we take."

"I don't think I wanna take it. Anyway, if there is gold down there it belongs to them pore wimmen down there whose men got kilt."

Kane's forehead wrinkled as he looked at Foulard in disbelief.

Foulard's chin dug into his left shoulder. "I mean it," he said. "If you lemme have that Indian pony I jes' believe I'll head out West, go to Californy or some place."

"The Indian pony belongs to you," said Kane.

"Well, I thought I'd ast, anyway. An' you'll lemme have a few shells fer my gun."

"So you can shoot me in the back?"

"Aw, fer hell sakes! Whatever made you say somethin' like that there?"

"Because you're that kind, Foulard," said Kane. "You was so hungry to get here you took risks you'd never dream about otherwise. Now you expect me to believe you'd move on. . . ."

"With or without shells fer my gun I'm leavin'," Foulard said.

"Get on your horse and ride," said Kane, and turned back to his task.

"If that's how you feel I won't go."

"Suit yourself. But if you're staying, take all three horses up to the next little box canyon. They've grazed out that place where they are now."

Foulard left sullenly and silently.

Working in the hot sun, Kane had almost all the stone he'd reuse when Juanita came around the corner of the church carrying a basket. There was a gaily colored cloth covering the basket. She was wearing a huge straw hat which she removed as she leaned against the church wall, shaded from the hot sun.

She smiled, showing her white teeth, all the whiter for her full, naturally red, sensuous lips. Her hair, black as a crow's wing, was pulled back and fastened, cascading to her waist.

He put on his shirt.

"I brought food," she said, "and I wish to warn you of danger."

She slid to a sitting position, her back against the wall, tucking her skirt around her legs and flipping the cover from the basket. There were slices of melon, half-dried grapes, half an orange and a few pieces of cheese.

He sat beside her as she held the basket toward him. He picked up the grapes. "Warn me about what?"

"They came last night," she said. "I hear them prowling. I know them to be Apache. I can tell by the odor they leave."

"What do they look for?"

She shrugged. "The people from beyond the mountains, with soldiers and others. These strange people pry in the ruins and violate the remains of those long dead."

"The ruins they pry into are those of another race, not related to the Apache. Why should the Apache be upset about this?"

"That I do not know." She rose to her feet, a lithe, catching movement, turning toward a sound.

Maurine Summers came around the corner of the church stopping abruptly at the sight of them. She wore a flat-crowned black hat, a velvet vest over a white silk blouse and a split riding skirt. Her highly polished riding boots were stained with dust. She held a basket in one hand. She swept off her hat with the other, fanning herself, smiling at Kane.

"I brought you a picnic basket," she said gaily, "but I see your friend got here before I did."

Kane felt a warmth come over his face. "Miss Summers, Juanita Gonzales," he said. To Juanita, he spoke in Spanish: "This is the lady from beyond the mountains."

Juanita lowered her head. She spoke so softly Kane leaned forward to hear her. "Please have Ramon and Felipe return the basket." She walked rapidly around the corner of the church.

Maurine laughed nervously. "I'm sorry if I interrupted anything—"

"You interrupted nothing," said Kane.

She laughed again, this time spontaneously. "She's a very pretty girl."

"Some of them are."

"She's part Indian?"

"Perhaps, I don't know. I've met her only once—twice."

She considered his responses and adroitly changed the subject. "You're very generous, repairing their church. I'm sure Father Caldero and his flock appreciate it."

"It's something to do while I rest for a bit."

"You've come a long way?"

"Not as far a distance as you've come."

"That should put me in my place." She smiled. "You're good at that. Maybe I'll learn." She hesitated, her red lips parting and then closing. "I suppose you'd—no, I guess not. I'll give this lunch to Lieutenant Jay."

"Why are you here in dangerous Apache country?"

She flushed and fanned herself with her hat. "I—I was getting too serious about a young man in Washington, D.C. My father thought this trip would make me forget. He arranged it."

"You didn't have to come."

"Yes, but I wanted to. I wasn't too sure about the young man I mentioned. I've since decided that my father was wise."

Kane thought of his own father, nodding. "Usually they are."

"Was your father—"

"My father is dead," said Kane.

The set of his face sent a swift rush of sympathy coursing through her. "Oh, I'm sorry."

"He was a good man," said Kane. "A stonemason. That's how I know how to lay stone." He felt impelled to tell her more, that perhaps his actions had caused John Kane's death, that through his deeds, the lives of a number of people went awry. He was not a man given to impulse. A private man, he kept his feelings to himself.

"You seem so competent," she said. "I'll bet you can do anything you set your mind to do."

"That's saying a lot." He looked out toward the village, waving his hand. "Those women down there, alone, they need more help than I can give. The little garden patches they depend on, they must carry water to irrigate because the ditches are all filled. It would be good if the gate, the water gate, could be repaired, the ditches cleaned."

She only looked at him, a puzzled frown wrinkling her smooth brow.

"Perhaps you could get the Army to help do it," he said.

She nodded agreement, her face smoothing out. "I'll ask Lieutenant Jay. He always co-operates. The soldiers, yes, and the others have time on their hands."

The pact, simple thought it was, seemed to draw them closer together. They looked at each other, loath to part. She repeated, "I'll certainly mention this to Henry—Lieutenant Jay, that is."

After she departed it seemed to Kane that her presence remained, the odor of her, the touch of her warm hand on his arm, the look in her eyes. He labored through the long, hot afternoon, working, sweating, and all of it seemed good. He didn't think once of the ghosts pursuing him.

Within a day's ride from Armijo, Jake Lugo, the civilian scout for Lieutenant Jay, carefully scanned the canyon leading to Nantana's valley, unaware that this was near the Apache hideout. He was not too concerned about this surveillance that had been ordered by the young lieutenant who'd hired him on as civilian scout. Jay was an ignorant man, Lugo thought, so far as Indian lore was concerned. Lugo had nothing but contempt for the youthful officer, a feeling he had carefully concealed. He thought he'd find a shady spot and sleep for a few hours before returning to camp to report to Jay that no hostiles were in the area.

Lugo turned his horse toward the shade cast by a towering boulder when an Apache lance pierced his chest, penetrating his heart and emerging beneath his shoulder blade. He fell soundlessly, his horse whinnying, shying sideways and spilling the scout, who was dead when he touched the ground.

Talin, one of Nantana's most trusted allies, who had scouted the Summers' camp, came from behind a giant saguaro and squatted over the dead man. Talin scratched his head, recognizing the hated Mexican who worked for the Army. He took two quick strokes with his knife and removed the black bushy tuft of top hair. He took Lugo's guns and ammunition, rigged an ingenious device to Lugo's saddle, hefted the man into the saddle and lashed him securely with Lugo's own *reata*. Talin then stripped the bridle from Lugo's horse and whipped the animal into a run.

He mounted his pony and continued up the canyon to report to Nantana, as he had things of much interest to discuss.

An hour later Talin was seated beside Nantana in the latter's camp, telling the Apache leader of his observations of the past few days.

There was a deep and enduring relationship between these two, friend and ally. He and Talin had been together at the big massacre in Chihuahua, when the Mexican authorities tricked, slaughtered and attempted once and for all to wipe out the Apache. Nantana had lost his first wife and two children. Talin had lost his father and mother and his wife and baby. They had been together most of their years, welded by a mutual hatred of Mexicans and Americans.

Hugh Giles squatted nearby, digging another mescal pit for Delores, the Mexican wife he'd saved from banishment when Nantana went through the ceremony of divorcing her to take a young wife. Giles often wondered what had happened to the young girl. He'd not seen her since the first day here.

Talin leaned over the cooking pot and sniffed at the contents. He looked at Nantana. "You live well, brother," he said.

"Nantana is the Apache's greatest leader," he said, nodding. "Help yourself to what you will."

The pot contained the rarest of delicacies: a stew made from cow fetus. Talin shook his head. "Food will dull my mind and tongue," he said. "I have much to relate. On my way here from the white-eye camp I killed their scout. These are very strange people, Nantana, foolish, eating, drinking and carousing."

Nantana nodded. "I shall go down and kill all of them one fine day."

"I should be with you." He glanced at Giles. "I do not see why you keep this one."

Nantana felt reluctant to discuss the matter with even his closest friend. The truth was, he had a deep conviction that Giles could bring him luck. But he could not tell Talin. He said, casually, "He's a brave man and tough. Also, he's a good worker. Forget him, Talin. Tell me more of the white-eyes from beyond the mountains."

"There are seven soldiers, five drivers and five men who help them, several slaves who wait on the two women and—"

"Women?"

Talin nodded. "One is much respected by all the others. She must be an important person. The other is old but not wrinkled."

Nantana nodded encouragingly.

"There are twenty-four mules, twenty riding horses, much ammunition and many guns. And there is fire-water."

"Why are they here?"

Talin shook his head. "Two of them, with help of the others, dig in the ruins, where the Ghost People lived long ago."

Nantana frowned. "That is bad," he said gravely. "Very bad."

Talin nodded agreement, his black eyes glittering. "I have even greater news, Nantana." He stopped, savoring the sudden deepening interest of Nantana. He went on, "I know that Cashis, the greatest shaman of our People, of the Coyoteros, is coming to join you. He is on his way here at this very moment."

Nantana's eyes narrowed. He would welcome Cashis,

of course, for he'd long felt the need of a medicine man to further his plans. He guarded well his power, which was secure now, due to his victorious forays of recent days. But that power could fade, he realized, like smoke in a high wind. The shaman, especially one of Cashis' reputation, might pose a threat to his control of the warriors with him at that moment. "That is good," he said.

"I thought you'd be pleased," Talin said, rising. "I must be on my way, Nantana. I liked watching white-eyes, especially since I know that eventually we will kill them all."

Nantana also rose. "Do you think the white-eyes are searching for gold?"

"That I do not know, my brother," Talin said.

"You know the trouble the gold always brings. The crazy white-eyes will do anything for it."

Talin nodded. "Many of our people have become slaves and died for it."

"Without doubt the gold is cursed and must not be touched. If brought out of the dark it would only bring sorrow and much bad luck."

"I do not believe this bunch is searching for gold," Talin observed. "Two of these who seem to be the main ones prowling in the ruins make marks in little books and talk considerably, conferring with one another." He hesitated. "There are two new whites, who camp below the church. I do not understand why they are here." He described Kane and Foulard in detail. "It may be that these two are looking for the cursed gold."

Giles, digging at the mescal pit, stiffened as he eavesdropped. He recognized Talin's description of Foulard and he had trouble controlling his sudden convulsing rage. Foulard was responsible for his predicament. He stifled his anger, listening to the two Apaches.

"Something else, Nantana," Talin continued talkatively. "I hesitate to tell you this but one of the others, a very tall, dark-skinned man, resembles you to a great degree. I have also seen a talisman such as the one you wear around this man's neck." He leaned forward and touched the pendant suspended from Nantana's brown muscular neck. Nantana moved his body back, so that Talin would not touch his charm, which was a source of power to him.

"Impossible," Nantana said. "There is no other like this, Talin. You should know that."

"Of course I have not seen it up close," Talin said, "but it surely resembles the one you wear."

"*Hi-ya!* I must look into this. I must see this man you describe with my own eyes."

"When you wish to go you know where I will be." Talin strode to his pony, leaped astride the animal and rode back toward the entrance to the valley.

Hugh Giles's rage was replaced with elation. He'd listened to the conversation and only now realized that he'd understood most of what these two said. He was learning fast.

Or was it fast? He'd lost all track of time.

"Lazy Americano!" Delores shrilled from the wickiup. "Bring me more firewood, dog! The fire is going out!"

"*Si, señorita,*" Giles said meekly. Didn't she know he'd saved her worthless skin?

CHAPTER 9

At daybreak Jared Kane slipped away from camp, crossed the rugged malpais to the small valley where the animals grazed. The black gelding whickered and minced toward him, while the Indian pony and mule bolted away.

Despite the urge to get on with the start of the tunnel, Kane saddled the animal, mounted and headed for the creek. The black had lost the gauntness imposed by the desert. Now it needed exercise. A horse not used grows soft and Kane never knew when the condition of the black might mean the difference between living and dying.

The horse was not thirsty, so he turned upstream and came at last to the Summers' camp. Maurine came from her tent as he approached, smiling a glad welcome.

"You're in time for coffee," she said. "Jeffrey just made a fresh pot." She motioned him to the ground.

Beyond the tents he could see five troopers currying their horses while the civilian teamsters lounged around the fire laughing and talking. As Kane watched, Lieutenant Jay came from his tent where the guidon was flying, glanced toward them and then headed toward his soldiers. Activity increased as Jay neared his troopers.

Kane stepped to the ground. "I'm exercising my horse," he said. "Where are the professors?"

"Off to their digging, of course," she said. "Mrs. Canfield is indisposed this morning." She gave him an inviting look through lowered lashes, smiling a caress that shook him.

"I counted only five troopers," he said.

She shook her head in mock vexation. "You miss nothing, do you?"

"Nothing so plain as six horses to be curried and only five soldiers at it."

She pointed. "The missing soldier."

Kane turned to see a mounted trooper posting toward Jay's tent. Seeing Jay, he swerved his mount past the tent and trotted to the lieutenant, dismounted and saluted. While the soldier and officer talked, all movement ceased among the soldiers. Then there was a concerted yell and all five troopers tossed their kepis into the air, joined hands and danced in a whooping circle.

"For goodness sake!" Maurine exclaimed.

Jay came striding toward them, a smile on his young face. He gave Kane a soft salute and spoke to Maurine. "One of my troopers just brought word from the village chief, Señor Gonzales. Seems the great event of the year is about to happen. Abraham Katterman is coming!"

"Who in the world is Abraham Katterman?" Maurine asked.

"He's an old peddlar who comes around a couple of times a year, bringing goodies to the women and children. Seems he adopted the villagers a couple of years ago, after all the men were massacred."

"That's very nice of him," Maurine said. "They celebrate his coming?"

"Exactly. When Abraham gets here everybody celebrates. A fiesta, *baile*, or whatever. We've all been invited." He glanced at Kane. "And you too, sir, with your partner."

Something else to slow things down, Kane thought irritably.

Jay bowed slightly and turned away toward where his troopers chattered excitedly.

"You don't seem overjoyed," Maurine said.

"I hope Jay doesn't take all his men away and leave the camp unguarded," Kane said.

"Oh, he wouldn't do that. Wait until I saddle my horse. I'll ride down to the village with you."

"Let me do it," Kane said.

While Kane saddled her horse, a mettlesome red mare, she disappeared into her tent. By the time the cinches were tight she emerged wearing the split skirt and blouse he remembered, fastening on her flat-crowned black hat. He helped her into the saddle and the feel of her warm, rounded arm beneath his fingers sent unaccustomed juices flowing.

They rode down the trail, circling the mesa on which the church stood, Maurine talking constantly, about the country, the people, the Mexicans and Indians.

The tinkle of bells heralded Katterman's arrival. The traveling merchant, an elderly man with a luxurious black beard streaked with gray, sat on the seat of his jump-seat wagon which had been modified to meet his needs of hauling merchandise around the rough country. His wagon was drawn by a big-footed draft horse, the like of which was seldom seem west of the Mississippi River. The bells, attached to the edge of the top of the open wagon, gave off a melodious sound as the vehicle jounced over the rough road leading into Armijo. Children attached themselves to the wagon and followed it along. Women waved from their jacals as Katterman passed. Kane and Maurine fell in behind the wagon and followed it to Gonzales' hacienda, where the old man waited, wearing faded finery, flanked by his two sons and several of his grandchildren.

Kane and Maurine dismounted under a cottonwood and held their horses while they watched the gathering crowd.

Old Gonzales made a flowery speech and by the time it was ended the entire village of some fourteen women, twenty-six children, several burros, goats, sheep and chickens were assembled before Gonzales' hacienda.

Katterman presented Gonzales with the money he had collected on his rounds, given to him by the miners, farmers, trappers, prospectors and soldiers with whom he had come in contact during his travels. Afterward, he presented the girls with dolls and the boys with pocket-knives, and then the women surged forward for their calico, mirrors, ribbons and whatever Katterman had collected. He even had a bottle of painkiller for the oldest lady in the village, Dona Portales, reputedly over a hundred years of age, even more wrinkled than Gonzales, whom she referred to as "my son."

Afterward, Ramon and Felipe Gonzales disappeared to prepare the barbecue pit, where goat and sheep would be cooked for the festivities. Katterman was led to the cottonwood by old Gonzales and introduced to Kane and Maurine.

Kane learned that Katterman owned a general store in Prescott but twice a year hitched his horse to the traveling store and made his rounds, selling goods to gold hunters, farmers, ranchers and to the soldiers at isolated army posts. He sold knives, tobacco, belts, shoes and boots, ammunition and even parts of army uniforms. After the Armijo massacre, he made it a habit to stop at the village with the goods and money he'd collected for the widows and orphans. He had come to be regarded as the villagers' patron saint even though all of them were devout Catholics.

The villagers dispersed and Kane and Maurine, at Gonzales' invitation, sat in the patio, infected by the air of excitement that surrounded the town. Kane saw Foulard standing before one of the jacals and he excused himself and walked down to accost him.

Foulard looked around, startled, when Kane spoke.

"What's all the fuss about?"

"The peddler Father Caldero mentioned. The old merchant brings things to the women and children."

"Whatever the hell fur?"

"He feels for them, I suppose," Kane said. He looked curiously at Foulard. "Don't you know anything about that?"

"Why, sure I do. I remember I took keer of ol' Pete Trawler in his last days." He peered at Kane. "Don't you believe me?"

"Sometimes I wonder," Kane said. "Shouldn't you be at our camp?"

"Aw, hell no, I'll miss all the fun."

"I wouldn't want anyone snooping around there."

"Hell fire! Everybody's gonna be here. Even the soljers." He nodded with his chin.

Lieutenant Jay and his troopers rode in the forefront of the teamsters and scouts as they swept down into the village. In a moment the soldiers had dismounted, tethered their horses in the cottonwood grove and mingled with the natives. The teamsters and scouts wandered aimlessly through the dusty street. If they get to drinking and fighting, Kane thought, there'll be trouble.

"All right, Foulard," he said, "but keep an eye out toward our camp from time to time. I'll do the same." He spoke to Foulard's retreating back and watched for a moment as Foulard joined a circle of spectators watching two young boys with fighting roosters preparing their birds for battle.

He returned to the patio and found Father Caldero had joined the group. Father Caldero took pains to let Katterman know that Kane had repaired his church. The darkhaired merchant nodded approval, but his words were for Father Caldero.

"Juan Perez and his wife—er, fiancée, Inés—beg you to come as soon as possible for a wedding. If you do not hurry there will be a baptism of the new baby along with the wedding."

"The priest nodded. "I have thought of them often. Living so far from the village must cause them much inconvenience. What do you find around the country in your travels, Mr. Katterman?"

"The Indians are moving around. I hear that great numbers are leaving the reservations and joining Nantana. The Army, under General Crook, is preparing to make war against them."

Father Caldero made a sign of the cross. "I will pray for peace," he said.

As evening came the smell of barbecue filled the air. One of the women brought a *bijuela*, a great primitive harp, and Ramon played the guitar under the soft sound of the wind in the cottonwoods as night came down. As the two played the soft music of lonely shepherds, the villagers and guests grew quiet.

Kane found Juanita beside him. She wore a rebozo Abraham had brought over a close-fitting gown of black and white lace. She looked up at him with black lustrous eyes and with the smallest motion of her head led him away into the gathering dusk. She walked ahead, down between rows of corn that grew between two jacals, until they stood on the edge of the murmuring creek that circled the cluster of huts. She turned and put her warm fingers on Kane's arm.

Kane could hear the faint sounds of the harp and guitar floating down on the cool night air.

"The drivers who work for the lady—they are molesting one of the village women—"

"The soldiers?"

"No, not the soldiers, the rough ones who drive teams and the others. I fear she will be hurt, Jared."

"Show me where," he said, and followed her past the rustling corn stalks, to where she turned into a jacal at the end of the garden. As he neared the jacal he could hear a woman scream and he broke into a trot. He came to the door, breaking through a cluster of four or five teamsters and entered the jacal.

"Hey there, feller, it's not you turn!" one of the teamsters yelled.

"Yeah, hell, git to the end o' the line."

Kane went into the jacal and for a moment he couldn't see. Then he made out the struggling forms of a teamster and a woman. He made it to the man in two swift steps and yanked him away, whirling him around. The girl pushed herself against the wall and began adjusting her clothing.

"What the hell's the matter with you?" the teamster snarled and threw a haymaker at Kane, a blow that landed on his shoulder, staggering him. The teamster whipped out a knife and started for Kane with the knife outthrust, the point tilted upward.

Kane jerked out his Colt and thumbed back the hammer. "Drop the knife," he said, "or I'll blow a hole through you." He was looking at a square-built man with a lot of hair on his face, pale gray eyes, a red bandanna around his thick neck and a wild look about him.

"I said throw it down," Kane said, raising the gun.

The knife thudded on the packed-earth floor.

Kane holstered his gun and stepped forward and slammed his fist against the big man's jaw, knocking him back into the wall.

The teamster roared, put his head down and charged like a maddened bull. Kane stepped to one side and his fist lashed out, catching the teamster alongside the head and knocking him to his knees. He staggered to his feet and charged again. Kane met him head-on, with a crashing blow full in the face. Blood and spittle flew in Kane's face as the big man crumpled to the floor.

A ring of faces in the doorway looked from the fallen driver to Kane and back again. "Heck fire! That feller done knocked ol' Laxton plumb unconscious!"

"Get him out of here," Kane said.

The three men came in and one of them got on each side of Laxton and lifted him to his feet. The other man leaned over to pick up Laxton's knife and then looked at Kane. "All right if I take Laxton's knife?"

"Take it," Kane said.

The man grabbed the knife and followed his fellow teamsters out into the night.

Juanita came into the room, her dark eyes large and liquid. She was trembling as she came and leaned against him.

It all seemed so natural to Kane. She tilted her head and her red lips were slightly parted. He put his head down and kissed her and her arms circled his neck and the next kiss was fierce and brief.

"I hope I'm not interrupting anything," Maurine Summers said from the doorway. "Someone said there was trouble here. I didn't know—" She stopped speaking, her fair skin flushed. She brushed back her hair and calmly replaced the black hat. She turned away and ran through the door.

Kane said, "I'd better explain," disengaged Juanita's arms and followed Maurine. She wasn't in sight when he reached the roadway fronting the jacal. He stood there uncertainly for a moment and then there was a pound of flying hoofs and Maurine flashed by with her horse in a dead run.

He sighed and turned toward the grove where his own horse was tied. He mounted and rode his horse at a walk toward the Summers' camp. The people in the patio had gone inside and the sounds of a waltz floated out to Kane on the cool night air. They were dancing inside the hacienda. It looks like a large fine night, Kane thought gloomily, for everyone except me.

He rode slowly, his thoughts mixed, but uppermost the memory of Juanita's warm body against his, of the sweetness of her lips. He turned it all around and remembered the look on Maurine Summers' face as she stood in the doorway.

He passed the teamsters, still supporting Laxton, without speaking and rode on, faster now, apprehensive that the darkness was not lighted by the usual large campfire Maurine insisted on as a nightly ritual.

Impossible, he thought; Jay would not have left the camp unguarded. But it appeared so.

He rode near the wagons and stopped his horse, his apprehension growing at the silence. Up near the ruins a coyote howled, ending on a quivery note. "Me, too," he muttered, and got down from his horse.

Maurine's horse stood nearby, sides heaving from the furious gallop from the village.

"Maurine," he called.

There was silence for a long moment and then a piercing scream came from the nearest tent.

Kane's boots dug into the ground and he ran toward the tent to be met by a hurtling dark form striking him in the chest and knocking him sprawling on the ground. He smelled Apache even as he saw the flash of the knife reflecting from a pale rising moon. He threw up his hand, grabbed the wiry brown wrist and twisted. It was like trying to hold on to the wind. The Apache turned, writhing, kicking, biting and struggling to free his knife hand.

Kane rolled, still holding to the knife hand, rolling over and over and coming out on top, savagely kneeing the Apache, desperately twisting a wrist that had grown slippery from sweat and grease. He lost his grip, flinched as the knife flashed and he felt the bite of steel. The man bounded away, disappearing into the darkness.

By the time the rest of the party returned to camp from the village, Kane had a fire going. Maurine had fainted when confronting the Apache in her tent. She attempted to care for Kane's wound, which was only a skin-deep slash across his chest. She rested now, in the collapsible chair, regarding him with a steady gaze. She was pale but composed.

"You saved my life," she said. She frowned, wrinkling her fair forehead. "I owe my life to you, Jared."

He shook his head.

"If I owe you my life what do you owe me?"

"Nothing," he said and turned away into the dark.

CHAPTER 10

Kane drew a diagram in his notebook of the proposed tunnel from the base of the mesa near their camp, estimating the upward slant to a planned ending under the church, hoping the end would reach the chamber containing the gold.

If the gold was there.

"What's it all about?" Foulard asked, peering over Kane's shoulder.

"Our route to the gold."

"When we gonna start?"

"Right away."

"How soon?"

"When it's dark."

There was a hail from the bluff and Lieutenant Jay waved at them and began descending the narrow steep path toward them.

"What the hell does he want?" growled Foulard.

"We'll find out." Kane put away his pencil and notebook as Jay approached and gave Kane a soft salute.

"Good morning, Mr. Kane." Jay smiled. "Miss Summers asked me to contact you. I'm only too happy to be of any help in your project."

"Have a seat," Kane offered. He sensed that Jay was being more friendly, perhaps to atone for leaving the camp unguarded.

Jay seated himself on a boulder Kane had rolled in for just such a purpose. The officer removed his hat, took out a handkerchief and dabbed at his face. "She mentioned something about cleaning out the irrigation ditches. How much time do you estimate this job will take?" He quickly added, "Not that we haven't plenty of time."

"Not more than a couple of days."

"I must keep four of my troopers on duty with the professors," Jay said. "But you can have the other two. Also, you're welcome to the civilians—the teamsters, hunters and—"

"Hunters? You hired hunters?"

Jay nodded. "Fine hunters they are," he said scornfully. "The only time they bring back game is when Lugo goes with them to show them how it's done."

"Lugo? He's your scout?"

Jay nodded. "A good one, too. He's out now, checking on the unusual Apache activity you mentioned."

"Do you still have doubts after last night?"

Jay flushed. "Perhaps I erred."

"I'll buy that," Kane said dryly. "When will Lugo be back?"

"I don't know really. But he's very dependable and will return as soon as he gains the intelligence he's after." Jay rose to his feet. "Where'll I have the men report?"

"At the head of the irrigation ditch," Kane said. "We'll start there and clear all obstructions from the creek to the fields. We'll rebuild the water gate, too, so the water can be diverted from the creek."

"As you wish," Jay said, raising his hand and turning away.

Kane and Foulard watched Jay as he climbed the steep path to the mesa top, which he managed to do without losing his military bearing.

"What'd you wanna know about Lugo fur?" Foulard asked.

"It's important to know all that can be learned."

"You make me feel stupid," Foulard growled. "I don't give a fart about anything but gettin' that gold and gettin' outta here."

"If we're not careful we'll be buried here," Kane said.

Hugh Giles watched Delores squatting over a mescal pit, taking out the sticky lumps of cooked agave. Not only was mescal food but it provided a feeling of well-being, Giles had discovered. Not that he got very much; but he'd grown to like the sweet molasses flavor of one of the staples of the Apache.

"Bring firewood," Delores commanded without looking at him.

"I just brought a load," he said.

"Bring more. Now. Or I'll tell Nantana and he'll beat you."

Giles got up wearily and started up the creek. He'd lost weight and was weak but he'd never given up hope.

He had to range farther and farther to find firewood. The Apaches were gathering, increasing daily. Giles went behind a clump of rocks, circled around and looked back on the *rancheria*, marveling at the size of it from the first day he'd arrived. He shrugged. Only more competition for firewood, from the squaws. It seemed to him that he spent most of his days gathering firewood and lugging it back to camp like a pack mule.

He turned and made his way to the creek and walked upstream, wading when the stream wandered, until it narrowed and squeezed in until it was barely a foot wide. He'd never been this far away from the *rancheria* before. After the first week or two, hardly anyone paid any heed to him as he ranged far, looking for wood, or gathering century plants for processing. He was reasonably certain there was no way out of the valley except through the narrow pass below the *rancheria,* which was always well guarded at the mouth of the canyon leading into it as well as along the way and at the entrance.

The valley was huge, circular and sloped gently upward, to where the forest of pines grew all around. Above the pine, rugged perpendicular walls shot upward toward the sky. He stood, surveying the rim, as he always did when not under the eyes of the Apache, seeking a way out, always seeking.

He carefully surveyed the rim, turning slowly until he had made a complete circle. It was the same as always. There was simply no way out without a rope—or wings.

Giles knew he was in trouble. He'd found trouble much of his life but always before he'd been able to cope with it. This was different. It would take everything he'd learned from the day he was born to escape from the Apache, to live and to go on to find Foulard.

He broke away from the creek and walked slowly to the edge of the pine trees, listening to the sigh of the wind passing through. Beyond, a fallen pine, struck by lightning or felled by high winds, gave promise of a load of wood. He walked on the slippery pine needles until he came to the tree, where he methodically began breaking off the limbs, tossing them in a pile which he'd gather in his arms when he had a load to lug back to Nantana's wickiup. He had not machete, or even a piggin string to hold the wood together.

When he estimated he had all the wood he could carry, he stooped to wrap his arms around it, and from that vantage point low on the ground, he saw the red rock of the bluff making a prison of the valley. He tensed, dropping the wood but remaining stooped close to the ground. Through the brown pine trunks he could see what appeared to be a rift in the wall.

He ran up the incline, an eagerness filling him. At the base of the sheer wall he stopped, puzzled. He'd lost what attracted him in the few minutes he took to reach this spot. He swung back and forth, casting about for the rift or fissure in the rock that had attracted his attention. He leaned back, tilting his head, looking upward where the sun fell full on the rock wall. He saw it then, his eyes following it downward, toward the base of the wall. He went ahead, his heart beating wildly, and stopped, putting his hands in what was a crack, looking up, seeing where the crack widened and deepened, until at about fifteen or twenty feet the fissure was deep and wide enough to hold a human body. His body.

If he could reach the fissure higher up, he was certain he could get into the crack, and with his back against one side and his feet against the other, he could literally walk out of the valley.

What lay beyond he didn't know. He decided he'd face that when he got to it.

He started up the cliff face, hanging onto a ledge here, a knob there, clinging to the face of the rock with his hands and feet. His moccasins helped. He was drenched with sweat and his breath came quickly. He was frightened, too, the higher he climbed. He tried to wedge himself into the fissure but it was too narrow at this point. He rested but not for long, steeling himself to go on.

When he was high enough so that he could wedge himself into the fissure he was too tired to go on. He squeezed and tried to relax, knowing he had to get his strength back in order to make it to the top.

He looked upward, seeing the blue sky. The rim of the bluff seemed as far away as the sky.

He didn't know how much time elapsed before he

began climbing again, using his back and his feet, inching up the cliff face, a bit at a time.

It was nearly dark when he climbed over the rocky rim, and lay helpless, exhausted, unable to move. But he felt a sense of victory that was sweeter than anything he'd ever experienced before.

Kane watched the unbelievable sunset, with the splash of purple and red clouds as the sun settled beyond the distant rim. Shortly after dark he began digging into the near vertical wall at the base of the mesa, well away from the trail used by many of the villagers to get to the church. He found the earth to be of tough clay but the work went faster after he'd penetrated a few feet into the ground. He loaded the excavated dirt into the woven baskets the Gonzales brothers had left. Foulard carried the basket to the crevice and dumped it into the narrow ravine.

They worked steadily through the night, taking only short breaks, and the tunnel deepened. Kane's knife cut across the chest started bleeding again but he worked on. When the sky began to lighten over the eastern peaks, Kane emerged from the shallow tunnel.

"Let's clean it up," Kane said, putting away the pick and shovel. He erased as well as possible all sign of their activities. He completed it by placing brush over the mouth of the tunnel.

Foulard slumped against a boulder. "Oh, lordy," he said.

"It's not perfect," Kane said, standing back to survey the area. "It'll have to do."

Foulard crawled, exhausted, under the canvas shelter. "God, just let me die," he groaned.

"We haven't even started."

Kane ate and then washed in the creek. His chest was sensitive but when he scrubbed off the blood it seemed to be healing nicely. He returned to camp and roused Foulard.

"Let's get moving. We've got to repair the irrigation ditch while we've got the Army to help us."

Foulard crept out from under the shelter and stood up, stretching and scratching. "We can't work night and day," he whined.

"We'll live through it."

"Who wants to when there's nothin' but damn hard work and misery?"

"You'll get hardened to it."

Foulard buried his face in his two hands. "How'd I ever get mixed up with you?"

"You've a short memory, Foulard. You would've died out there at that water hole if I hadn't come along."

Ten men were gathered at the old water gate when Kane and Foulard arrived. None of them appeared to be happy over their detail. The troopers had ridden over and their horses grazed nearby. The teamsters and their helpers had walked, as had the two hunters. The scout, Lugo, seemed to be missing as Kane scanned the group.

The teamster Laxton, with his ruined face and two black eyes, glowered at Kane but said nothing.

Lieutenant Jay smiled, nodding at Kane. "We're all present and accounted for," he said cheerfully, oblivious to the discontent of his soldiers and civilians. "They're all yours, Kane. Don't work them too hard." He gave them all a bright smile and departed, his shoulders squared as usual.

"Stack your rifles over there," Kane directed and

watched them as they carelessly placed their arms in a pyramid. He gave instructions, quickly and clearly, and the men listened and then silently fanned out, each with his task to do. Soon the sounds of their picks and shovels filled the air. Down below, small knots of women and children stared upward at the activity between the village and the bench mark where the ditch had originally branched from the creek to divert water to the village fields.

The two troopers worked on the very old water gate made of logs, which in the distant past had been used to dam the creek and divert water to the irrigation ditch. They argued quietly about how to do the job best: throw away the old gate, which was waterlogged and rotten, and build a new gate from the stand of young pine in a narrow canyon nearby.

Kane settled it for them. "Replace the rotted logs," he said. "Use as much as you can of the original gate."

The younger trooper, Zeke Burden, nodded. "That's how I wanted to do it."

The other, an older man whose faded shirt proclaimed he'd once been a corporal, grunted. "It's all the same by me," he said. "But you'll have to decide which ones are too rotten to use."

Dr. Porter Canfield drifted down the creek and waved to Kane. He was wearing a white shirt, riding pants and knee-high lace-leg boots. He brought two cigars from his shirt pocket and offered one to Kane.

Kane shook his head. "No, thanks."

"Your Mormon upbringing, no doubt."

"No, smoking is simply a nuisance. Sometimes, out on the trail, one runs out of the weed. Then it's just another want to be filled."

Canfield nodded agreement and lit his cigar. When it

was going to his satisfaction he gestured at the irrigation ditch leading down to the village fields. "This irrigation system is at least a hundred years older than the United States," he said. "Those ruins Flannery and I are poking around in—the inhabitants constructed it about the time Attila the Hun laid to waste Thrace and Illyria."

"How can you tell?"

"A guess, admittedly, but an educated one. Why they abandoned the low ground to hole up in their cliff house is beyond me. Perhaps some predatory force, such as the Huns—"

"That may be the time the Apache moved in."

"Possibly." Canfield nodded. He took out his watch, looked at it and then at the sky. "I'd better get back to the dig."

The workers were spread out along the ditch, cleaning out the tumbleweeds, dirt and rocks that had caved in. A buzzard sailed overhead in the blue sky and in the far distance a few white clouds drifted before the wind. All seemed peaceful as the dust-brown bodies appeared suddenly from the canyon spreading into the sloping meadows above the village. Kane, sprinting for his rifle, saw young Burden fall to the ground. The men along the ditch were running toward him intent on reaching their guns. Kane stood, spread-legged, taking careful aim, caught up the slack on the trigger and squeezed off his first shot at a fleet-footed Apache. The man buckled at the knees and pitched forward. He shot slowly and deliberately, picking out elusive targets, as Apache braves darted from cover to cover. His fire was deadly.

The teamsters and the others had reached their weapons now and they went into the ditch, firing over the bank, down into where the Apache seemed to be concentrated; only fleeting glimpses could be seen of the darting warriors.

One of Jay's hunters lay sprawled where the rifles had been stacked, victim of an Indian bullet before he could bring his gun into action. An older man, a teamster, was inching his way toward the ditch, favoring a wounded leg when an Apache bullet ripped off the top of his head.

A man yelled from across the creek, "Perfesser Canfield done got it!" followed by a string of blistering curses.

As suddenly as it started, action stopped. All at once, as though a hand had swept them away, the Apache disappeared.

Sweat trickled down Kane's cheeks and dripped on his shirt. He found that somehow he'd gone to his knees on the bank of the ditch but he didn't remember getting there. The buzzard was gone. The sky was empty except for a few clouds. His knees hurt and he shifted his position and brushed away the rocks biting into his flesh.

Cashis, the Apache medicine man who led the attack on Kane's work party, sat back, puzzling, after waving his braves off. His original intent had been only to join forces with Nantana. After the fight he squatted, alone, gazing up the mesa, where the white-eyes had congregated around the big man who fired his rifle with such accuracy. Cashis, above medium height, but appearing shorter because of his great depth of chest and width of shoulders, was truly puzzled. He wore his eagle feathers, his medicine shirt and had made the proper obeisance to the spirits, yet his attack failed under the best of conditions.

It was his instant rage, he reasoned, when he saw the intruders opening the ditch, that caused him to fling his braves into battle. The ditch meant something to the hated Mexicans in the village. Too, these white-eyes were working with picks and shovels and he thought them to be unarmed.

Cashis was a long-headed Apache, with a fine brow and an eagle beak of a nose and thin, cruel lips. He had gained such a reputation as a medicine man that even the great Nantana sought his council.

Now, Cashis thought gloomily, he'd made a mistake, both a tactical and strategic error which bothered him enormously. He lifted his rifle and lance and silently faded into the scrub oak, going straight as the crow flies to the prearranged rendezvous with his band, including the squaws and children they were escorting to Nantana's *rancheria,* when he stopped to make the foolhardy move against the white-eyes. Cashis smiled bitterly, thinking he'd better caution his braves to say nothing of their abortive fight.

He'd lost six good braves. Now and then he could hear the muted wails and moans of the bereaved women and children.

It was nearing sundown when Cashis and his party reached the *rancheria.* Nantana himself came to meet them and immediately sensed something wrong. Upon entering the enclosed hidden valley, the squaws in the band had given full vent to their sorrow. The entire camp turned out to extend sympathy and threats of retaliation and vengeance filled the air.

"The ditches that water the fields are being opened," Cashis announced. "I thought we'd put an end to that once and for all."

"They are foolish to bring down our braves upon them," Nantana replied. "The white-eyes are strange ones, indeed. They will never learn, it seems." He had other things on his mind as he led Cashis to his own wickiup and ordered Delores to bring food and drink.

When Cashis had eaten, Nantana leaned back on his elbows, watching the young boys throwing their lances at a rolling hoop. Aware of his gaze, the youngsters excelled in the sport. "I need your help, Cashis," Nantana said. "The white-eyes camped near Armijo and who dig in the ruins of the Ghost People are very rich, have many horses, mules and other things the crazy ones seem to enjoy. Talin has told me of this and will make it easy for me."

Cashis turned his head so Nantana would not see the narrowing of his eyes. "I don't trust Talin," he said flatly. "He has scouted for the horse soldiers. He is no longer of the People but more like one of the whites." He spat.

"Talin is true to us, to me," Nantana said.

"What is it Talin wants?"

"He wants nothing but to kill white-eyes and take their guns and horses. We need these things to fight the soldiers."

"Are you sure he doesn't want the gold of the iron shirts.

Nantana was silent. He'd never considered that Talin wanted anything from him. Talin had been his friend, his confidant, his spy, and all of this was because he was Nantana's friend. Nantana shook his head. "Talin wants no gold."

"The gold is cursed," Cashis said.

"Suppose Talin did want gold. You have the medicine to take away the curse. The yellow stuff means nothing to us, Cashis. It's the mark of the white-eyes who are mad for it." He looked Cashis in the eyes. "You may have your choice of any loot we may take for your help."

Cashis leaned forward and placed a brown finger on the blue and gold pendant suspended from Nantana's neck. "I would have this for making strong medicine, nothing else," he said.

Nantana stiffened, his nostrils flaring, his eyes flashing. "Cashis, this, as you know, has been given from father to son of my line for generations. I do not know how old it is but it may be as ancient as the People themselves. I cannot do it."

"I'll need it to make medicine strong enough to take away the curse of the gold," Cashis said with finality, rising to his feet.

Nantana looked after the retiring Cashis and fingered the pendant suspended from his neck. It had brought him through many battles, many victories, he reflected, protecting him from the bullets of the soldiers and others who would kill him. He'd feel naked without it, and yet Cashis might even extend the powers the pendant offered.

Delores came to squat beside him. "Giles the Grayhair has not returned from fetching wood," she said.

"Waagh! Bring me tizwin, woman!" he ordered. Maybe this was a sign that he should give Cashis the pendant. He felt the need of the feeling tizwin gave him, to help him make up his mind.

CHAPTER 11

The campfire made their shadows dance on the ground behind them as they gathered in the Summers' camp. Maurine came from the Canfield tent, stepped into the circle and walked carefully around the fire to stand beside Kane.

"She's resting," she said. "Maybe she'll sleep."

Prince Luis looked up from cleaning his rifle. "Is good," he said.

In addition to Canfield, those dead were the young trooper Zeke Burden, who'd been shot through the heart, a burly teamster named Edgerton and Clay Addison, one of Jay's hunters.

Kane watched the Spanish prince working on the mechanism of an expensive rifle.

Lieutenant Jay resumed his speech, which had been interrupted by Maurine's return from consoling Mrs. Canfield. "You understand my first duty is to Miss Summers," he said. "I refuse to mount pursuit of those savages and leave this camp unguarded."

Prince Luis' lip curled in a humorless smile.

"There's no question in any of our minds," Flannery said testily, "about your responsibilities." He sipped brandy from a snifter. A half-empty bottle of brandy stood on the ground beside his chair.

Jay's troopers and the civilians were standing together

for once, on the outskirts of dancing firelight, listening intently, saying nothing.

"We better settle with them for they'll be back," Flannery continued. "More of them next time." His words were slurred.

Kane decided Flannery was almost drunk. It troubled him because now, more than ever, clear heads were needed. A moment later, he suddenly realized that Flannery was grieving for his friend and colleague, Canfield. The two men had been close, he'd observed.

As Kane spoke all heads turned toward him. "I believe this raid was a—an accident. A small band moving from one place to another for whatever purpose."

Prince Luis raised his head and looked intently at Kane but said nothing.

"The Apaches fight and run. And when they run it's as though the ground swallows them up. But they're near—when they want to be."

Foulard sniffed, and said, "We'd better git back to camp, Kane."

"You may go when you will," Prince Luis said, speaking to Foulard but looking at Kane. "When I'm ready I will go after these savages whether anyone else goes or not. It matters little to me." He patted his rifle stock.

"Don't do anything foolish, Prince Luis," Kane said quietly. "The Apaches are part of this country. They know it better than you know your own castle—if you have a castle."

"I've made my decision," Jay said with determination. "The moment Lugo returns I'm sending him to the fort with a report—" He stopped speaking as the clear voice of a sentry reached them.

"Halt! Who goes there—God Almighty, Lieutenant!" The challenge turned into a scream of pure terror. A bridleless horse trotted to the edge of firelight and stopped, its head drooping.

The rider swayed in the saddle. The odor that came from the horse was unmistakably of death itself.

Lieutenant Jay said in a quivering voice, "Soldier take that horse a quarter mile from here and wait. All of you go with him!"

The soldier pulled his neckerchief up around his nose and led Lugo's horse away, with Lugo swaying drunkenly in the saddle. The civilians followed reluctantly.

Kane estimated the man had been dead for at least four days, maybe five.

Kane and Prince Luis sprang toward Maurine at the same time. Kane reached her first and scooped her in his arms as she fell. He carried her to her tent. Prince Luis hurried ahead and lighted the lamp. Kane laid her her on the bed.

Prince Luis said, "You may go now. I will take care of her."

"You go to hell," Kane said coldly and strode to a table holding a water pitcher and bowl. He poured out water from the pitcher into the bowl and dipped a cloth into it and went to the bed and sponged off Maurine's face while Prince Luis silently glowered.

Kane remembered this tent, the soft rug, the luxurious appointments, from the time he'd fought the Apache. And let him get away, he reminded himself grimly.

Maurine stirred and opened her eyes. She looked up at him, her eyes widening. "Oh, Jared! How horrible!"

"Forget it if you can," he said. "There's absolutely nothing you can do. Lugo hired on as a scout. He knew the chances he was taking. It's not your worry."

"But he was such a funny man, always saying amusing things and making everyone laugh. To be treated in such a brutal and savage way—" She shivered and closed her eyes tightly.

"Everything the Apache have done to us," Kane said, "we've done to them in spades."

"Are you defending those murderous savages?" Prince Luis demanded angrily.

"They need no defense," Kane said. "Apache ears hang from almost every barn and jacal in the territory. The Mexican Government paid a bounty for Apache scalps, men, women and children. Scalp hunters were so active, anyone with long black hair wasn't safe, not even the Mexicans themselves."

"Hah! You're telling one of your Yankee tall tales."

"Not at all. It started with Fray Marcos, *your* countrymen, Prince Luis. While looking for gold, he either converted or killed all he contacted. Coronado—"

"Do not presume to give me a history lesson," Prince Luis interrupted.

Kane smiled coldly and stood, looking at Maurine. "I hope you'll feel better soon," he said. "I've got to get back to my camp." He moved toward the door.

Maurine said, "Wait, please."

Kane halted, turning to look at her.

She sat up in bed and said, "Leave us, Luis. I wish to talk to Jared—alone."

"Very well, señorita," Prince Luis said curtly and strode out of the tent.

"Now he's angry," Maurine said. "I don't care." She sat up and swung her feet over the edge of the bed and invited him to sit beside her.

Kane reluctantly sat on the bed, waiting for her to talk, as she plainly intended to do.

"So much has happened," she said. "I feel I'm a very different person from when I first met you."

He nodded. He found her exciting, even more so now than before.

"Down at the celebration at Mr. Katterman's reception, when you kissed Juanita—"

"It just happened, I can't explain it."

She gave a secretive smile. "You don't have to explain, Jared. There's nothing to explain."

"The teamsters were molesting one of the village women. Juanita asked me to help and I did. After I fought with Laxton, the teamster, and got them out of there, it just happened."

"Are you in love with her?"

"I don't know," Kane said.

She seemed relieved. "I'll be leaving here soon," she said. "I hate to think about it."

"Lieutenant Jay is upset," she went on. "He depended a great deal on Lugo. Now Lugo's gone and Henry is at his wit's end. You could help him."

Kane shook his head. "The Army has one rule—don't let the civilians interfere with military operations."

"I could convince him," she said.

"Please don't. I'm not in a position to help Jay run his squad. Or make decisions."

She frowned. "I know what will happen. Henry will send a courier to report to General Crook. I'll be leaving and I hate the idea. I do feel safe with you near."

He slid off the bed, rising to his feet.

She stood also and placed her hand on his arm. Her hand slipped down from his arm to clasp his hand. He was aware of its warmth. . . .

"I'll keep alert," Kane said, "and come if I'm needed." He returned the pressure of her hand and resisted the impulse to stay there, to be with her, for the excitement she brought to him. He moved to the entrance of the tent and stood there for a moment, watching the group around the fire. He had no inclination to join them, even for a moment. There was an air of gloom about them that he wanted to avoid.

He stepped out into the darkness and circled to avoid going near the fire. He was irritated that no sentry challenged him as he made his way toward his own camp. He was poignantly aware of Maurine as he walked through the night, listening to the night sounds—an owl hooting, a coyote howling, the sweep of the wind over the rugged terrain.

Suddenly there was a movement beside the trail. He stopped, grabbing swiftly at the dark outline. It was a woman. He released Juanita.

"It's a bad thing to be out here alone."

She stopped closer to him. "My father is frightened. And very angry."

"Can't say as I blame him."

"He says the trouble comes from the eastern people digging in the ruins. He also thinks you're after Spanish gold. He would have all of you go away."

"We will go soon."

"Take me when you leave," she begged. "I want to go with you, Jared Kane."

"What would your father say to this?"

"He would be grieved."

He took her arm and guided her along the dim trail. A coyote howled from a distant peak and her flesh quivered beneath his fingers.

"You don't know me, Juanita," he said quietly. "Why would you go away with a man you know nothing about?"

"I trust you."

"Do you trust everyone you meet?"

"No. But you are different. You care for people. I can tell."

"Feelings are not always to be trusted."

"I cannot stay here, Jared Kane. There are only the women to talk to. Nothing happens, nothing at all."

"Nothing happening is better than bad things that come to one."

"I'd risk it."

They came to the church, skirting the walls, and went down the steep, narrow path. She walked before him and he kept his hands on her shoulders to catch her should she stumble on the rough path.

Foulard was not in camp. Kane assumed he was at work in the tunnel. He said, "I'd better walk with you to your house."

Without looking at him, she said, "No!" and was gone, a shadow in the night like the whisper of wind in the scrub oak and tumbleweeds.

Kane stood there, feeling the brush of the wind against his face, thinking of Juanita, running through the night; perversely, at that moment he visualized Maurine Summers. He shrugged off these clashing thoughts and images and went along the base of the mesa to the tunnel entrance. The moon was on the far side of the sky, outlining long, slender, horizontal clouds. He could hear sounds now, of Foulard working deep inside the tunnel. He knelt before the barrel-size entrance, seeing the dim flicker of the candle up the slight incline to where Foulard worked.

Kane judged the tunnel to be halfway to the underground chamber beneath the main portion of the church.

If the map is true, he reminded himself.

The rope attached to the basket jerked and Kane began hauling on it. When the basket reached the mouth of the tunnel, Kane untied the rope on Foulard's side, gathering up the rope he'd hauled the basket out with, and lifting it all, walked to the crevice and upended the basket, hearing the rattle and swish as dirt slid down the steep sides of the crevice.

Back at the tunnel mouth, he secured the rope to the basket, jerked on it and the basket moved slowly into the tunnel as Foulard took up the slack.

The sound of Foulard's pick came faintly to him as he knelt again in the mouth of the tunnel, waiting for Foulard to reload the basket.

It was slow work. The sound of Foulard's pick stopped. The scuffle of the shovel came faintly to him. They had to cut off the handle to work in the narrow confines. The work was hard, not from digging or shoveling, but from the close confines of the tunnel, which cramped all but the smallest movement.

A rush of air and a frightened, smothered cry came to Kane. He stiffened, feeling a sudden prickling of his scalp. There was a momentary stirring within the tunnel, almost like the sighing of a wind, but the wind had died away for the moment. The candle no longer flickered.

Kane scrabbled into the tunnel on his hand and knees. "Foulard," he called softly.

There was no answer, nothing.

Kane felt his way in the black hole, perspiring now, when he felt his way barred by a wall of dirt.

The tunnel had collapsed.

Kane began digging at the dirt with his hands. Foulard had the only shovel and Foulard was buried somewhere beneath the dirt of the cave-in.

He thought of going for help and rejected the idea at once.

Hugh Giles evaded the Apaches once but he knew from the intensity of the search and the numerous search parties that it would be only a matter of time until they caught up with him. Unarmed, in hostile country and afoot to boot, he felt the vulnerability of his present status.

He now lay on a ledge, a dozen feet above a rocky trail, holding his only weapon, a ten-pound boulder, in his hand. He'd seen the lone Apache take to the trail leading to a mountain saddle up above and he hoped, nay prayed, that the Indian would pass beneath him.

Through the night and all this day Giles had run and hidden and run again. He had no way to carry water and was suffering from thirst. Sucking pebbles did little to help. He could hardly generate a drop of spit.

But if he could manage to drop this rock on the brave at the proper time he could get weapons and a horse—and water. The thought of water made him thirstier than ever.

He lay perfectly still, waiting expectantly for the sound of the pony on the trail. From where he was stretched out he surveyed the country around him, rugged, broken by arroyos and much of it covered with desert plants. He knew approximately where he was but didn't know how to find the two men Talin had mentioned to Nantana.

Giles was an adventurer, an opportunist, a man without scruples. It wasn't that he was good or bad, simply being an amoral person. He had been head guard at Yuma Territorial Prison, after an up-and-down career as an officer of the law, interspersed with periods of banditry, bounty hunting and scouting for the Army. He hungered for money and when the opportunity presented itself in the person of ex-outlaw Pete Trawler, he quit as head guard, put Foulard into Trawler's cabin and sat back to wait.

Foulard betrayed him and Giles took to the trail with his son, Bud, whose mother had been a crib girl in Prescott, and Zack Morton, a man who Giles trusted as much as he trusted any man. Not much.

Giles counted the score against Foulard and found it heavy. He'd lost his only son, a matter he'd not dwelt on since it happened. Death was a constant in this country. He lived with it casually and without undue concern for his safety. Most of his recent troubles rested on Foulard's shoulders, the way Giles looked at it. And he'd collect.

He knew he'd find Foulard eventually and settle the score. He'd killed men before and it mattered very little to him that he'd add Foulard to that list. He looked forward to it with some anticipation. But first the gold.

He heard the soft scuff of unshod hoofs on the trail and he tensed, grasping the boulder and shifting his body so he could drop his primitive missile where it would do the most good, preferably on top of the brave's head.

He rose to his knees as the pony neared, raising the heavy rock. The pony, sensing something unusual, whinnied and shied. The rock sailed harmlessly past the brave, hit the edge of the trail and bounded out into space. Desperate, Giles launched himself toward the brave, who was in the process of raising his rifle. Giles crashed into the brave. The force of his falling jump drove the pony to the ground where it squealed, kicked and struggled. Sprawled over both horse and man, Giles's huge hands encircled the brave's neck, suqeezing with desperation. The terrified horse thrashed about until it freed itself from the two men, but all the while Giles continued to squeeze even after the man's tongue protruded and he ceased to breathe.

Only the pony struggling to its feet caused Giles to drop the Apache. He leaped to his feet, grasping at the trailing rawhide fastened to a hackamore. The pony reared and Giles jumped, clasping the head, hauling it down with sheer brute strength, holding on and being dragged until the pony's struggles gradually subsided.

Giles talked to the animal soothingly, disappointed that it was small and rather scrawny.

He hung on to the pony with one hand and got the brave's knife and rifle. The man's pouch turned up only a half-dozen .44 caliber shells for the rifle and a few odds and ends, including luck pieces and a trifling article of jewelry the brave had gotten in some raid. He threw away all but the shells. Taking the Apache moccasins and putting them on his bare feet, Giles mounted the pony and continued up the mountain.

He'd have preferred going back down the mountain. That was the shortest way to Armijo. But he was afraid of running into more Apaches.

It was good to be riding again, even a poor mount such as this one. More important was the large intestine of a mule filled with water that had been tied to the horse's side. He gathered strength as he sipped and rode.

The sky was faint gray over the mountains when Kane helped Foulard to his feet outside the tunnel. There was enough light for Kane to see that Foulard was more frightened than hurt.

Foulard removed his shirt and shook out the sand. He removed his pants and boots and got rid of the sand and dirt and slowly dressed.

"Damn, I thought I was a goner," he said.

"You ran into a sand pocket," Kane said. "We'll shore it up and hope we don't hit another one."

"I'm not goin' in that damn hole agin," Foulard said flatly. "Not for no damn gold 'er nuthin' else!"

"I'll make coffee."

Kane stirred up the fire, added a few sticks of mesquite and, taking the coffeepot, walked off into the growing light, noting the formation of fantastic colors in the east.

He wanted to be away from Foulard, away from the stark fear and the smell of a scared human being.

He dipped the pot into a deep backwater of the creek, heard the soft gulp as the container filled, and he straightened up, listening. The only sounds he heard were the call of an owl, hooting softly from upstream, and the cooing of unseen doves in the willows beyond the creek.

It was near here he'd first met Maurine Summers. He thought of her with a detachment that had been missing the previous evening.

Back at the fire he placed the coffeepot on the bed of coals. He left Foulard squatting morosely by the fire while he went to the tunnel mouth and surveyed the ground around the opening. In his haste to get Foulard out he'd dirtied the area much more than usual. He used a pine tree top to clean around the tunnel mouth. He threw the pine top into the opening and replaced the mesquite covering, hiding the tunnel entrance. He wasn't satisfied but it was the best he could do at the moment. He turned and walked back to the fire.

Foulard was hunkered down watching the dancing flames. He glanced up at Kane. "If that'd been you in there I wonder what I'd have done."

"I hope you'd have got me out."

"S'funny. I dunno. I keep gettin' these quare notions that I ain't never had before I met up with you, Kane. I can't figger you out nohow."

Kane threw a handful of coffee grounds into the pot, noting that it was the last of his supply. He was running out of just about everything. He was sure that Gonzales would not provide him with more supplies.

Kane considered the scarecrow of a man across the fire from him. Foulard had changed subtly, somehow. He took a bath now and then without arguing. There had been other signs, not all of them bad.

"I ain't had much bringin' up," Foulard went on. "Out in the world at eleven or thereabouts. People took advantage o' me and my ignorance. If I'd had your bringin' up I mighta turned out better."

Kane had no feeling that he'd had any special advantage growing up. Life had not been easy on the Garnett spread where there was so much work to be done and nobody spared. There had been that closeness with his father—until John Kane married Christine Garnett and Preston arrived almost a year to the day later. Jared was seven years old then, when Pres was born, but he still remembered the excitement that attended his half brother's birth.

The world, his world, had changed from that day forward.

Maybe, he thought, just maybe I'll forget about it someday. He thought perhaps his growing search for the gold was based on his desire to make it on his own merit. Certainly, it would give him a base to buy a ranch, or to do whatever he wanted to do. He knew the cattle business inside and out. That would be the logical way to go.

Foulard finished his coffee and went off to check on the three animals grazing in the nearby grass valley. They were waxing fat on the nutritive grama grass.

Old man Gonzales toiled up the slope and came into camp, puffing with the exertion of his climb. He looked old as the rocks around them. His face was a wrinkled brown, eroded and dried to a mummified mask, with his two bright dark eyes to enliven it. His hair, long and straight, held not a trace of gray or white.

After greetings were exchanged, Gonzales seated himself on a boulder that was beginning to shine with use. "These are bad times," he said.

Kane agreed that the times were bad, waiting for the old man to finish.

"The fighting, the death. We still mourn our dead and now there's apt to be even more."

"Maybe not."

"But there will be." He lifted a frail arm and pointed to the mountains. "The smoke is there. Day after day. The enemy prepare. O, that none of you ever came here to Armijo. We had enough trouble without you."

"I will go soon."

Gonzales moved his thin shoulders. "That all would go," he said gloomily. "That would be good news. Maybe it is too late. The Apache are restless, more than usual. They love to kill and they are making ready to go on another killing spree. I hear the coyote howl and the owl hoot and it is the Apache telling one another things they know about."

Exhausted, Gonzales stood up. "Talking about it tires me out. I know not what to do. Perhaps I should talk to the good father. Yes, I may do that. He is out in the valley today for a wedding and a christening. He may know what to do, with God's help."

"In what way might I help you?"

Gonzales shrugged expressively. "Who knows? My only daughter, Juanita, looks on you in a manner that troubles me. O, that my old age should see so much trouble." He hobbled away, striking at the ground with his stick, a fragile man with trouble.

Foulard returned to camp as Maurine Summers hailed them from the top of the mesa. She waved and then came down the steep path, running at times.

She stopped when she was close, her face flushed with her exertion—and excitement.

"You'd better come, Jared," she said. "There's a man named Hugh Giles who just escaped from the Apaches. He says a large number of them have banded together and are getting ready to go to war."

Kane picked up his rifle. He looked at Foulard. "You coming?"

Foulard shook his head. He felt sick at his stomach but he didn't want Kane to know. "Nope. I'm stayin' right here."

CHAPTER 12

As Kane and Maurine walked, hands touching, into camp, Lieutenant Jay broke off from his troopers and civilians and strode toward them. He was grim-lipped, his youthful face troubled.

"I sent a trooper to Fort Defiance," he said crisply. "I'm afraid he's dead. His horse returned with blood on the saddle."

"You're apt to lose your first command before this is over," Kane said. "This *is* your first, isn't it?"

Jay nodded, looking crushed, and Kane had a feeling of sympathy for the young officer.

"We'll be all right, Henry," Maurine said soothingly. "I'd rather my father didn't know about all this. He'd worry needlessly."

"Ma'am, I'm here to protect you," Jay said. "I've lost three troopers just when I need every one of them. The general must be informed of what's happening. I'm bound by duty and direct orders to keep General Crook informed."

"What about the man Giles?" Kane asked.

"Flannery is interrogating him," Jay said. "In his tent."

Kane moved toward Flannery's tent and Jay followed, almost trotting. "I wanted to talk to Giles but Flannery took him away from me," he complained.

Reaching the tent, Kane called, "Professor Flannery, may I come in?"

"By all means," Flannery answered.

"I'm going in, too," Jay muttered and followed Kane into the tent.

Flannery sat at a small portable desk with papers spread out on it and a pencil in his hand. A shaggy-haired bearded man sat on the carpet that been spread over the ground. He was shirtless, his body brown as leather. His pants were ragged and dirty and he wore Apache moccasins.

"This is Hugh Giles," Flannery said, waving his hand toward the frightful-appearing apparition sitting there staring at Kane. "He escaped from Nantana day before yesterday."

Giles nodded. He held an empty glass in his hand. Flannery leaned down and lifted a brandy bottle and refilled Giles's glass and then replenished his own. "Drink?" he asked Kane.

Kane shook his head. "That's about the last thing any of us needs, Professor."

Flannery chose to ignore that. Instead, he asked Giles, "You were telling me that the Apache do not eat bear meat. Are you sure?" He scribbled on a piece of paper that contained much scribbling.

"Professor, I appreciate your interest in the Apache culture," Jay said, "but I need to question this man about Apache war plans."

"This won't be long," Flannery said, scribbling faster than ever. He looked at Giles with upraised eyebrows.

"Well, like I told you," Giles said, "Nantana went through this ceremony of divorcing his wife, Delores, so he could take the new girl, a young one. I recognized the divorce ceremony as something he'd picked up from the Cheyenne. So I asked him—"

"Nantana seemed to be well traveled, then?"

Giles nodded. "He'd been around. Smart buck, he is. Speaks American, Spanish, beside his Apache palaver. He—"

"Flannery, perhaps you don't realize what we're up against," Kane said quietly. "Nantana is about to take to the war trail. We need to know what he's about. So we can make plans, if any are possible. I suggest you defer this line of questioning until we get other information that may affect the safety of this entire party." Without waiting for Flannery's response, Kane asked Giles, "How many warriors does Nantana have?"

"He's got a handful," Giles said. "I counted twenty-eight the day I got away. That doesn't count three Chiricahuas Nantana doesn't trust. Them three used to scout for the Army."

"How're they fixed for guns and powder?"

"Well, that's why Nantana's gonna hit your camp first. His scout, Talin, has told him there's lots of guns and ammunition for them here."

"When do you think he'll try to hit us?"

Giles shook his head. "He put a lot of bucks out after me. He just might track me here and not back off."

Kane looked at Jay. "Any questions you want to ask him, Lieutenant?"

Jay shook his head numbly.

"Then he's all yours," Kane told Flannery, only to discover that Flannery had fallen asleep.

Jay followed Kane out of the tent, a worried look on his face. "I've got to get a message through to General Crook at Fort Defiance, Kane. What do you suggest?"

"You get Mr. Giles rested up and outfit him, he'd probably get through if anyone can."

"Mr. Giles? After what he's been through I doubt he'd want to risk it."

"Giles is no different from anybody else," Kane said

dispassionately. "He wants to live, too. If the Apaches hit us—"

"I see," Jay said. "I'll talk to him after he recovers."

"What you'd better do is see that he gets outfitted and fed and get him on his way."

"I'll do that, Mr. Kane. I'll see to it right away." He turned back into Flannery's tent.

Kane joined the group about the fire, noting that Betty Canfield sat next to Prince Luis, who held her hand.

Kane was aware that Maurine had come from her tent to stand beside him. He felt her presence, as he usually did when she was near.

"This man, Giles, has just escaped from a group of Apaches headed up by one called Nantana. Giles says Nantana is planning to raid this camp. When, we don't know, but we may expect it anytime. Lieutenant Jay is aware of this and is making plans to send another messenger to the fort—"

"His last messenger met his death on the way," Prince Luis said sardonically.

Kane looked at the man, annoyed. This Spanish nobleman had a lot to learn about Apaches and Apache country.

"His last messenger was a raw recruit, fresh from the old country," Kane said. "He'd never have made it alone under the best of conditions."

"I resent that, Mr. Kane!" Lieutenant Jay said. He'd approached the group unobserved. "I do the best I can with what I have."

"I meant no uncalled for criticism," Kane said. "But it's in keeping, your action that is, in leaving the camp so poorly guarded. In fact, I suspect that if General Crook knew of that, he'd have your scalp. By court-martial, of course."

Jay flushed a deep red and kept his eyes toward the horizon. "I have no excuse," he said, "only regret." He wheeled and went toward his tent.

Kane took his leave of the people around the fire, noting their numbed looks, except for Narbona, who apparently was enjoying himself. He kept his rifle close at hand and was very attentive to Betty Canfield.

Maurine walked with Kane to the outer perimeter of the camp. "You're very severe with Henry," she said.

"He'll learn faster," Kane said.

She tugged at his arm, stopping him. "I wish you were here all the time," she said. "I'm depressed. And filled with a dread I don't understand." She seemed to be struggling with her thoughts and he had a sudden large feeling of wanting to protect her.

He looked down, between the mesa where the church stood and the bulge of the low mountains on the right. He looked at Maurine. Their eyes met and he looked quickly back down into the valley and moved toward his camp. But took only one step. "I wish I could be here all the time," he said. "But there's much to do. I'll be on my way in a day or a few days—"

"You'd leave when this Apache is preparing to attack us?"

"We don't know for sure," he said. "If I thought that Crook wouldn't or couldn't get soldiers here in a hurry of course I wouldn't go and leave you." He'd meant to reassure her but she gave it another meaning, he realized, as he saw a glad light appear in her eyes, on her face.

"In the event the Indians attack before Henry can get help?"

"Foulard and I would do our best," Kane said. "The best we could hope for—would be to stand them off." What he'd almost said was *we'd take a few with us*. He was glad he'd changed his words.

"What shall we do?" she asked.

"Lieutenant Jay is beginning to realize what he's up against," Kane replied. "With the teamsters and helpers and hunters, plus his three soldiers, he should be able to stand off Nantana for a time. Until help comes."

Even as he spoke he was thinking of how people rather than a place could be defended. There just wasn't any way to defend the Summers' camp. It was too open, pitched there with no thought of possible attack.

He thought of the church as a fortress. It was built of stone, the original structure, at least. The later addition was of adobe, walls two feet thick. A group of determined, well-armed men could fort up there and hold off an army, providing they also had food and water.

"Don't worry," he said, the words sounding empty even to himself. He took one last look before losing sight of her as he rounded the bend in the arroyo. She was still standing there, the wind whipping the skirt around her ankles. That picture of her remained in his mind as he strode on toward his camp.

Nearing camp, Kane heard the thud of hoofbeats, not of a horse running, but of a horse protesting. He broke into a trot and rounded the shoulder of the mesa and saw Foulard, in a flurry of motion and curses, trying to put a saddle on the Indian pony. The pony, tied to a boulder, circled with Foulard following, carrying the saddle.

"Where you going with my saddle?" Kane asked angrily.

Foulard stopped in the act of throwing the saddle across the back of the skittish pony, turned and dropped it.

"I gotta get outta here," he said. "Hugh Giles'll kill me sure as shootin' if I don't. I ain't about to git myself kilt."

"So you're stealing my saddle to ride out on."

"That danged Indian pony sure got a razor back," Foulard whined. "It'd cut me in two 'fore I got half a day from here." He brightened. "I din't try t' steal yore horse, I didn't."

"Saddle sores would be the least of your worries," Kane said. "The Apaches would have you staked out and burning in less than half a day."

"I'm more afeared o' Giles than I am them injuns."

"You'd better think about that some more," Kane answered. "And damn it, put my saddle back where you found it." He watched as Foulard lifted the saddle and carried it back under the tarp where Kane had placed it when setting up camp.

The wind sprang up, gusting, bringing dust and sand with it. A moaning sound came from the church on the bluff above, the wind playing around the belfrey, a sound that drowned out most other sounds. Kane caught a movement from the corner of his eye and he swung around sharply.

Hugh Giles stood ten feet away, holding the rifle with the scalp lock in his two hands, with the muzzle pointing at Foulard.

"Hello, Foulard," he said.

For an instant Foulard froze, his face gray, his mouth open. Giles loomed against the sky, still dressed in the ragged pants and moccasins, nothing else, his hair wild, his face relentless. The wind flapped his pants around his ankles.

"Come on in by the fire," Kane said.

"I don't mind if I do." Giles stepped forward, his face grim and purposeful, his pale gray eyes watching Foulard. He was thin and emaciated but there was a fierce resolve about him that caused Kane to move slightly to be in a better position for whatever might happen.

When Giles reached the fire, still looking at Foulard, he said, "I've come for the map. And to kill you."

"You raise that rifle," Kane said, "and I'll kill you."

Giles showed his teeth but he wasn't smiling. "Some have tried," he said easily, and then spoke to Foulard: "Well, Harvey, what's it going to be?"

"You're moving too fast," Kane said. "Foulard took care of Pete Trawler in his last days. He took him into his cabin when Pete was dying. Trawler gave him the map. It belongs to him."

"That what he told you?" Giles gave a soft chuckle. "Let me put you straight, Kane. Foulard didn't take Trawler in. Trawler took him in. I got Foulard out of Yuma prison, and I sent him to Trawler. Trawler was the one owned a cabin up the river, not Foulard. What Foulard did was to kill the old man and take off with the map. That's the straight of it, right, Harvey?"

So his name is Harvey, Kane thought.

"It ain't so!" Foulard shouted. "It's all a dad gum story he's cooked up. It's jes' like I told you, Kane, so help me God!"

"I'm not inclined to believe either of you," Kane said coldly. "Plain, somebody's lying. But wait—we're in one hell of a spot here, and fighting between you two won't help matters. If you try anything, Giles, it'll be a big mistake on your part."

"Well, I don't know. We'll see."

"It might be better for you if you made a deal with Lieutenant Jay. He needs your help."

"The shavetail? You tellin' me he needs help! All them dudes need help. But I come here through hellfire and brimstone for a purpose and I ain't about to let go."

"You'll get outfitted and food and supplies from the

Army," Kane said. "You won't get anything here but trouble."

"It looks that way," Giles said, looking about with a critical eye. "Mighty poor camp."

"Talking about hellfire and brimstone," Kane said, "when you ran into Nantana the first time you'd have been all right if you hadn't tried to chase him, run him down."

"So that was you?" Giles asked. "Fired that shot to warn me."

Kane nodded. "I tried to keep you from riding into a trap. It didn't work, Giles. You were too eager to kill a few Apaches."

"Yeah. Just think, I was that close to Foulard and didn't know it. But I know one thing—Foulard would never have tried to warn me if he'd been by himself."

Considering Giles, Kane didn't think Giles would have either but he didn't speak it. Giles was an unknown quality to him at this moment but Kane wasn't impressed by what he saw on the surface. Giles had the cold gray eyes of a killer. Kane was sure he'd kill openly or from cover, whichever proved easiest for Giles. Of that, Kane was almost certain. He'd encountered men like Giles before and he recognized the breed.

Foulard untied the Indian pony from the boulder. "I'm gonna take ol' split-ear back to pasture," he said, and led the animal away.

Giles watched him go with a glint of amusement in his pale eyes. He looked at Kane. "I'll be seeing you, friend," he said, and turned away, going back toward the Summers' camp.

CHAPTER 13

True to his word, Foulard refused to enter the tunnel again. Kane shored up the strata of sand with discarded timbers from the water gate. He worked inside, with Foulard at the tunnel mouth handling the basket, which was beginning to show the effects of hard usage.

Sweat trickled down his cheek. Kane doggedly kept at his work, thinking that if Giles would accept a job from Jay, matters might be eased. Even so, there was some disadvantage: Giles was good with a gun, no doubt. He'd he one man less if Nantana attacked.

If . . . When is more like it, he thought.

Kane worked on until a faint glow at the tunnel mouth warned him of coming daylight. He was ready to quit when his pick suddenly plunged into nothingness. Rank and musty air filled his nostrils. For a moment, kneeling in wonderment, with little avalanches of dirt falling around him, he couldn't believe he'd broken through.

He leaned forward in eager anticipation. The candle, his last one, flickered a warning. It was almost burned out. He shoved his hand into the hole made by his pick and felt around.

Nothing.

Pushing the dirt surrounding the small hole aside, he enlarged the opening, his heartbeat stepping up, thudding in his chest.

Grabbing the candle, he shoved it through the hole.

The flame flickered. He could see nothing, pressing his face against the hole beside his extended arm. The candle, in a tin can that had been perforated all around, was only a stub. He pulled his hand back through the hole, reached inside the can, burning his fingers as he gouged out the stump of wax and wick. He held the burning candle stub upside down, letting the wax drip on the outside bottom of the can. When a small puddle of wax had formed he stuck the candle into it and pushed the can back into the hole. The candle stub fell off, dropped down into the darkness and sputtered out. He cursed aloud in frustration.

"Kane, Kane, somebody's comin'!" Foulard sounded frightened, as usual.

Backing out of the tunnel, he grabbed the pine tree top and erased signs of work around the tunnel mouth. He hastily tossed the basket, rope and pine tree top into the tunnel and replaced the brush covering the tunnel entrance.

He walked into camp as Lieutenant Jay and Maurine came down the steep trail.

"The man Giles refuses to take a message to Fort Defiance," Jay began even before they reached Kane. "Unless Foulard goes with him." He gestured toward Foulard as he spoke.

"I ain't goin' nowhere with that jasper," Foulard said positively. "It'd be like—well, I ain't gonna do it."

Maurine looked at Kane appealingly. "Couldn't you convince him to go?"

Kane shook his head. "I can't ask him to do that, knowing what I know about the two of them. And I'm not free to tell you about it. I'm sorry."

Jay straightened his shoulders and the grim look on his

face deepened. "I'm afraid we'll have to get ready to move everything and everybody. I've no choice."

Kane could scarcely conceal his relief. "That may be your best course of action," he said.

Jay wrinkled his brow. "I'm forced into it," he declared. "I've heard rumors that my civilian employees are about ready to pull out. Without them it'd be difficult going anywhere."

Kane nodded. "I wish you well," he said.

"Is that all you can say?" Maurine asked. "I thought— well, I don't know what I thought really, but—" She stopped speaking as a shout came from the top of the mesa. All of them turned their heads. A trooper stood on the brink of the mesa, cupping his hands around his mouth, a dark blot against the morning light.

"Mr. Jay, Mr. Jay, the civilians are deserting . . . they're on their way now!"

Without excuses, Jay hurried toward the trail, bent on handling this latest emergency.

"Them buggers are gettin' outta the fryin' pan right inter the fire!" Foulard shook his head.

Maurine looked at Kane for a long lingering moment and started to speak, then closed her mouth and turned away.

At the base of the mesa she turned toward him. "I'm sorry," she said. "You don't belong in Washington and I don't belong here. I hope—I wish you happiness, Jared."

She began climbing the path leading to the mesa.

Kane felt a regret and sadness he couldn't explain. He watched her out of sight and came back to the present to find Foulard had disappeared. He looked and saw him sneaking along the trail toward the village, keeping to the sage and the willows along the creek.

He'd been there more than once, Kane knew, and it angered him because Foulard had promised to stay away from Armijo and the village's lonely women.

Pulled two ways, he abandoned Foulard to his own devices and climbed the trail to the mesa above his camp. It seemed serene and peaceful there, he thought, viewing the sweep of the valley. He stood near the walls of the church, looking into the haze of blue distances, a discontent on him he could hardly understand. Then he realized it came from his lust for the gold and his sense of responsibility for Maurine and her party. And then there was his plan to commit petty theft. And in a church.

He went along the portico and pushed open a door that bore the ax marks of ancients. He was inside the church now, an unearthly silence around him. The large main room was deserted and yet Kane had a feeling he was being watched.

God?

He carefully scanned the room, standing there just inside the door, on the hard-packed caliche, worn shiny by uncountable bare feet brushing against the ox blood that gave it a satiny sheen reflected by the uncertain light at the altar, where a candle burned, flickering anemically inside a blood-red globe.

Kane moved forward, his moccasins whispering against the packed clay of the floor.

He moved past the altar and stopped in front of a small table holding the candle and evidence of past candles. He looked around again and then self-consciously knelt on the split log on pegs placed there for that purpose. He knelt there for a moment, mindless, and when he rose he had a candle in his hand which he jammed into his pocket. He tramped unhurried toward the door, opened it and stopped short.

Kane hesitated a moment and then said, "*Buenos días, padre.*"

"Good morning to you also, Jared," the priest replied, a tiny smile tugging at his lips. "You feel the need of a devotional, no doubt. How many Hail Marys have you said?"

"I don't know about your business, Father."

"One need not know about it to seek guidance," Father Caldero said. "One needs only faith."

"Perhaps I have it—of a kind."

"No doubt. In that wicked gun on your thigh. And the black horse below who after a month of rest is in need of more."

"A man is a fool to travel without a gun in this country, Father. And my horse is in good shape. I'm leaving soon. Perhaps tomorrow." He gave the padre a level glance. "Good day, Father."

"Wait, Jared," the gentle voice of Father Caldero stopped him. "I'm not blind, my son. There are many things I've seen since you came here."

Kane waited expectantly.

"Of great importance is Juanita. She's a child."

"She is twenty. She's a woman."

"In some ways, yes. What would you do with her, Jared?"

"She wants to go with me when I leave here."

"So? Can you make a home for her, Jared Kane?"

"She believes that to be true."

"Perhaps. But you are a man who looks over his shoulder often, Jared. What will happen to Juanita when she's far from her people and you must run again?"

"The things I run from are in here," Kane said, and tapped his head. "She may help me as I could help her."

"This in your head, you must deal with it alone."

"Life is short," Kane said. "And I don't know yet if I'll take her with me."

Father Caldero's sigh filled the air. "I must talk to Gonzales about this." He looked long and hard at Kane. "There is one other thing, my son. The Apache, they are a resentful people, Jared. It takes little to make them think of protecting what they regard as sacred."

Kane thought of the Apache attack against the ditch workers, of the dark flitting shadows, the hoot of the owl and sharp yelp of coyotes. "The pony soldiers are paid to look out for them."

"Agreed. But it's an impossible task. The smoke is rising and the bands are gathering. I think I know why."

"The Apaches don't need a reason. They are filled with hatred and enjoy killing."

"According to your reasoning, yes. But they are fearful that someone will take the gold that has been cursed. Any who molests the gold will be cursed also."

Kane laughed.

"I didn't say I believed the legend," Father Caldero chided gently. "I simply repeated it. And strange things have happened here in the past."

"Thanks for the warning," Kane said and watched the priest walk away.

A fever of impatience was on him now that he was so close to the gold—if there was gold there under the church.

Foulard came from the small valley where the three animals grazed. He made a great display of returning to camp.

"'Bout outta grass in there," he said. "A few more days and they'll be breakin' out for better feed."

"We'll be gone by then," Kane said and watched surprise wash over Foulard's face.

"Whatta y' mean by that?"

"We'll be in there tonight, Harvey. We'll know tonight if the gold is there or not."

Foulard's eyes glistened and his hands trembled. "Damn!" He started toward the tunnel. "Let's get it now!"

"No, we'll do it the way we planned."

Foulard whirled, snarling, "Don't be tellin' me what to—"

Kane's hand moved and his pistol appeared. He thumbed back the hammer. "I've about had it with you, Foulard," he said.

"Don't point that gun at me," he croaked. "I know, you want it all fer yourself and you're lookin' fer an excuse to gun me down."

"I told you not to go to the village."

"Aw, shoot, Kane, there's this lady down there what likes me. An' I he'p her out now and then, like carry wood—"

"Stop lying."

"I ain't lyin', I swa'r."

"You've lied to me every step of the way," Kane said, and eased down the hammer on his gun and holstered it.

Foulard let out a long sigh and visibly relaxed.

"When we get out of here, Foulard, we split. You go your way and I'll go mine."

Foulard appeared ready to cry. "I alluz tried to do what's right—"

"The hell you have. You're a liar and a cheat. And I suspect that Giles might be right about you murdering old Pete Trawler."

"I ain't never had much chance," Foulard said miserably. "I guess I'm just a natural born liar. But I didn't kill ol' Pete."

"I'll take you a day's travel from here," Kane said evenly. "Then we split."

"I need you, Kane. I can't go alone, all by myself. The Apache—"

"That's your worry," Kane said and turned away, climbing the trail to the mesa. He watched the village for a while. The peddler Katterman's wagon was still standing in the cottonwood grove near the cluster of jacals that looked as though they were die tossed out by a giant. Nothing moved except the smoke wisping up from the communal baking oven. He circled the church to get a look at the Summers' camp. Prince Luis was stationed on the east, pacing back and forth, carrying his rifle. Flannery and Giles were on the west, but huddled in conversation and not paying particular attention to standing guard. At the point of the triangle he recognized Jeffrey, the cook, wearing a campaign hat instead of his usual tall white cook's headpiece. Jay and his troopers, Kane guessed, had gone after the civilian employees who'd deserted the party.

Maybe those civilians are the smart ones, Kane thought. He stood there quite a long time, waiting for a glimpse of Maurine but neither she or Betty Canfield appeared and he turned back to camp, not looking forward to seeing Foulard again but having no solution to that.

Kane walked his horse into the cottonwood grove where Katterman's wagon stood. The huge horse was munching fodder nearby and Katterman was busy greasing axles.

Kane stopped the black and dismounted. "Good evening, Mr. Katterman," he said.

Katterman nodded, rising from his task of jacking up the right front wheel of the jump wagon. "Good to see you again, Jared," he said. He was wearing a duster that covered his business suit.

"Don't let me stop you," said Kane.

"I've this one wheel left to do," he said, unscrewing the nut holding the wheel to the axle.

Kane dropped his reins and came forward and lifted the wheel off the axle and held it while Katterman applied black grease liberally to the spindle with a wooden paddle. When it was done, Kane replaced the wheel and Katterman screwed the axle nut back in place and tightened it with a wrench. He let the wagon down, took out the jack and stowed the tools in a box under the seat of the jump wagon. He wiped his hands as he talked casually of his travels around the country.

"That's quite a rig you have there," Kane said, squatting and looking at the underside of the vehicle. "Longer than any jump wagon I've seen."

"I had it made over," Katterman explained. "Simply cut it in the middle and spliced in a piece making it longer. I strengthened it with oak beams. And I got the kind of horse to pull the load such as I carry. Old Paladin"—he nodded toward the huge horse—"is easy to care for and we get along fine." Katterman jammed the wiping rag into the pocket of the duster and removed it and threw it across the wagon seat. "I didn't make camp this time," he said apologetically. "I'm a guest of Señor Gonzales. If I'd made camp I could offer tea and cookies Juanita baked for my return trip."

"I haven't time anyway," said Kane. "I came by to warn you that Nantana and his braves are ready to cut loose any time. A prisoner escaped from Nantana and warned the people up the creek."

"Yes, I've heard," Katterman said gravely. "But aren't the Apaches always on the warpath?" He glanced at

Kane. "I made my peace with them years ago. They let me cross their land and I don't bother them, either."

"That's a nice arrangement," said Kane, "as long as it lasts."

"I'll be leaving tomorrow anyway. It'll be a relief to be back at my store in Prescott. I'm getting too old for this sort of thing, Jared. This may be my last trip."

"The people here will miss you."

"Ah, yes. I also will miss them. I do not make much money on these journeys but it gets me out into the country and I learn what's going on."

"I wish you'd let me know." Kane's voice held a note of humor.

Katterman chuckled. "The country's changing, growing." He grew serious. "Gonzales told me of your repairing the church. It was good of you, Jared."

Kane shrugged. "We do what we can," he said.

"If only that were so," Katterman said sadly. "A man should grow with the country. I may start a new store in Tucson or perhaps the village of Phoenix. I suspect that will be where the greatest growth takes place in the years ahead. I have no family, Jared, to carry on my business. I need a young man, strong and innovative, to take over the store when I'm too old." He looked at Kane expectantly. "Would you care to join me?"

"I'm flattered," Kane said. "But my knowledge runs to cattle. I was raised on a ranch."

"I thought perhaps you had a higher education," Katterman said. "You appear as such."

"I was raised among Mormons," Kane said. "A lot of people look down on the Mormons because of the plural marriage thing. But there's more to them than that. The church leaders send out missionaries all over the world seeking converts. And those missionaries have done a good job of getting well-qualified men and women. For instance, in the rough little town nearest our ranch, there were university teachers, very well-educated men who enjoyed teaching. There were also skilled craftsmen, a tailor, shoemaker, surveyor. They came to Deseret from all over the world."

"Even if you're a cattleman you'd be able to function as I do in a very short time. Frankly, I'd prefer one of my own people but so far as I know I'm the only Jew in the territory."

"It would be exciting to take such a challenge. I do wish being a merchant attracted me. I thank you and I want you to know you've made me feel very good today." He walked to the black, lifted the reins and mounted. "*Adios*, Mr. Katterman. Have a safe journey."

Katterman nodded gravely. "And may you travel in peace," he said.

"It may be a good idea to warn Señor Gonzales."

"He has lived all his life here in this valley," Katterman said. "He needs no warning."

Kane nodded and put the black into motion.

He'd examined Katterman's jump wagon closely. If necessary he'd be able to use it as the half-formed plan took shape in his mind.

Nantana and his braves, twenty-four strong, streamed out of the hidden valley when the sun burst over the mountains in a glorious riot of color. He elected to leave behind four braves to guard the camp—and to watch the three Chiricahuas, whom he did not trust.

He led the band east and north, intending to circle the camp of the hated rich white-eyes. It was pure accident that he found Lieutenant Henry Jay and his three troopers conferring with the deserting teamsters a few hours' ride from the camp he meant to attack and destroy.

He motioned and his braves dismounted, turning their horses over to horse holders. In a moment, Nantana's braves had merged with the brush and brown earth as they encircled the intended target.

The fight was swift and savage. Nantana's braves set up a murderous fire and at the first round of shots most of the hated white-eyes were killed before they could even draw their guns. The Apaches made short work of the cleanup. Nantana would have liked to have had one of them for sport but that could come later.

They took weapons, ammunition, horses and mules and burned the wagons. When the flames were leaping, Nantana turned again toward the camp by the creek.

Only one man survived the attack. Ben Laxton, who had dropped off the lead wagon to answer a call of nature, was squatting in a sandy arroyo when the firing broke out. He hid in a coyote den until the Indians were gone and all was quiet.

CHAPTER 14

Kane crawled into the tunnel earlier than usual, the nearness of the gold pulling at him like a magnet. Inside, at the end of the tunnel, he lighted the candle he'd pilfered from the church. He put it through the hole he'd made the night before, his hand shaking.

"Is it there?" Foulard hissed from the mouth of the tunnel.

"I'm not in yet," Kane replied. At first he could see nothing. He moved the candle aside, the light dancing on the dark walls of the room. As his eyes adjusted he made out a coat of mail and an iron helmet to one side. And bones. All around the room was the dull white gleam of human bones.

He put the candle inside the perforated can, set it down and began enlarging the hole he'd made when he broke through to the chamber. When it was big enough, he squeezed through the opening and dropped to the floor. Straightening, he reached through the hole and lifted the can holding the candle and raised it over his head, looking around.

He stepped among the bones and passed the length of the large underground room. At the end, which was about twenty feet wide, steps led upward, steps hewn into solid rock. He went up the steps and examined the trap door that apparently led to the interior of the church. He backed down the steps and turned. Skeletons and Spanish armor lay between Kane and the furnace and stacked bars of gold. He went across and squatted there, sweat beading his forehead, looking at the retort where the gold had been smelted down, refined and poured into molds about one and one half inches by three inches. He lifted a bar, marveling at the weight of it. About five pounds to the bar, he thought. He scratched the bar, which was dark brown, rough, bearing the marks of the mold, thrilling at the bright mark his nail made in the dull, pitted surface. He carried as many of the bars as he could manage to the opening into the tunnel.

Hauling the wicker basket to the opening, he placed a dozen bars inside it and jerked on the rope. Foulard took up the slack and the basket, under heavy use for so long, pulled apart.

Kane gathered up the bars and placed them in the underground chamber, stacking them carelessly against the wall. Carrying one of the bars, he crawled into the opening and inched his way toward the mouth of the tunnel, where Foulard waited. The chill night air on his face as he emerged from the tunnel felt good. Foulard stood waiting.

"What happened?"

"The basket finally gave out," Kane said, rising and dusting dirt from his clothing. "We've found it." He thrust the bar of gold into Foulard's clutching hands.

Foulard giggled ecstatically. "What'd I tell y'? Didn't I tell the truth, hey, didn't I, huh?"

"I'll get my saddlebags," Kane said. "We'll use that to haul it out. We'll have to hurry it up to beat daylight. There's about sixty of the bars. I guess three hundred pounds in all."

"Three hundred pounds!" Foulard's voice broke and he

looked around apprehensively. "Three hundred pounds! God'l'mighty!"

"Bring up the mule and Indian pony."

"Gawd, I don't wanna leave it for a minute!"

Kane took the gold bar from Foulard and dropped it on the ground. "Go on, get moving," he said.

Foulard disappeared into the dark, mumbling to himself.

Kane retrieved his saddlebags from under the shelter and came back to the tunnel entrance, dumping them on the ground. He dropped to his knees to enter the tunnel when he heard the sound of horses. He rose to his feet, turning. Foulard had brought all three animals. He felt a warning signal from somewhere in the back of his mind. He'd have to watch Foulard closer than ever.

"We'll put about a hundred pounds on the Indian pony, say twenty of the bars. And the rest on the mule." He looked speculatively at Foulard. Sweat beaded the man's forehead and his hands trembled.

"We gonna light out soon's we load the stuff?"

"No. We got other things to do."

Foulard muttered a curse. "What's more important than gettin' this gold outta this Godforsaken country?"

"I don't believe we can make it," Kane said. "Nantana and his braves are everywhere. We wouldn't have a chance."

"Oh lordy! What we gonna do?"

"I have a plan and I think it'll work."

Suspicion was in Foulard's voice when he asked. "What kinda plan?"

"Abraham Katterman. I looked his wagon over. I think we can hide it so he won't find it. He'll carry it out for us, and then later on we'll pick it up in Prescott."

"The hell you say!"

"Yes. We won't have to worry about the gold while we help those people up the creek get back to Fort Defiance."

Foulard stared, his eyes bulging, his neck swelling.

"You gonna do what?"

"It'll be safe with Katterman. The gold that is. He has free passage through Indian country. We'll ride into Prescott when this is all over and pick up our gold. Katterman will never know he's carrying—"

Foulard leaped toward Kane's rifle, swept it up and levered a shell into the chamber. "You ain't throwin' away my gold you crazy—"

Kane heard the twang of the bowstring as Foulard screamed, dropped the rifle and tore at the feathered shaft protruding from his shoulder. He turned, still screaming incoherently, and fell to the ground, scrabbling for cover. Kane dived to the shelter of a rock with his pistol in his hand.

He could see nothing in the darkness around the camp but an arrow whistled by his head and lodged, quivering, in the rock beside him. He could hear Foulard groaning in the darkness.

From where he crouched Kane could look down into the village but no light showed. These poor people had no candles to waste. They went to bed when night fell and got up at daylight, except for special occasions. He swung his head and the outline of the mountain to the east came into his vision against the brightening sky. Still two hours to full daylight, he thought, and felt a sense of urgency invade him. As he watched, he explored the ground with his fingers until he encountered a small rock. He tossed it out into the darkness. Instantly something moved and Kane fired, hearing the thunk of the bullet, feeling it reach the mark from the pistol in his hand. There was a sound of a thrashing body, and then silence.

He waited, curbing his impatience. But as he waited he found it more difficult to remain still. He slid out from cover and bellied along the ground in a circling pattern, toward where he'd gotten in a lucky shot. He didn't want a fight but he had to get out from this camp before Katterman hitched up for the long drive to Prescott.

Kane wormed his way toward the huddled body of the Apache, came close enough to pick up the rank odor of the brave. He stopped still when he heard a scurrying sound but after a few tense moments he decided it was made by a lizard or pack rat. Foulard was quiet for the moment.

I'm crazy too, he thought, as he stood up, inviting an arrow. None came. He went to the Indian and checked for a sign of life and found only death.

Foulard groaned again and Kane went to him. He sat on the ground holding his arm. When Kane appeared he began to blubber, "Goddammit, get this thing outta me!"

The arrow had pierced the upper part of Foulard's arm, entering from the back, the flint-tipped missile tearing flesh but apparently not touching the bone.

Kane stared coldly at him. "You tried to shoot me with my own gun," he said. "Why should I take it out?"

"Dammit, you can't just stand there!" Foulard cried in anguish. "It ain't hooman!" He added plaintively, "Anyway, I wouldn't have shot you. I'd have died out there in the desert if you hadn't got me out."

Kane squatted beside Foulard and took out his knife.

Alarmed, Foulard said, "You ain't gonna cut it out?"

"I thought I'd take the arrowhead off and then pull the shaft out," Kane said, testing the blade on his thumb.

Foulard said nothing, but his face was pale and sweaty.

With his free hand, he gripped his pierced arm above the arrowhead. He blanched as Kane put the knife to the shaft.

Kane worked on the thin pieces of gut, skin or tendon that held the arrowhead to the shaft. Toughened by some Apache process, the binding, almost as if it were metal, resisted the blade. Kane kept picking away at the binding until it began to unravel. With each movement Kane made, Foulard flinched and gritted his teeth.

"Lucky it didn't hit an artery," Kane said.

"How kin y' tell?" Foulard whined. "Hurts enough for it t' be an artery."

"Color of the blood," Kane said shortly. "Hold still!"

The arrowhead fell to the ground, and with a quick motion Kane drew the shaft from Foulard's arm. The blood coursed down with each heartbeat.

"Oh, gawd, I'm gonna bleed to death!" Foulard gasped.

"Let it bleed for a while."

"You ain't got no heart."

"I've nothing to use to disinfect the wound," Kane said. "So if it bleeds quite a bit there's less chance of it festering up and maybe giving you blood poison."

"I—I stole a bottle of whiskey from the perfesser," Foulard said. "It's in my boots which I been using fer a pillow."

Both Kane and Foulard had taken to wearing moccasins since starting the digging.

Kane rose and went to their camp and quickly found the bottle of brandy. He also ripped an old shirt for bandages. He carried them back to where Foulard sat, holding his arm.

Upending the bottle, Kane let a liberal portion of the brandy flow into the wound while Foulard gasped and cursed.

Kane placed the bottle on the ground and Foulard seized it and tipped it back and drank heavily.

"That alcohol'll thin your blood," Kane said, "and you're liable to bleed to death if you take another drink."

"Oh, lordy," Foulard groaned, "you know too damn much an' you're always takin' the fun out of life."

Kane was silent, placing a tourniquet above the arrow wound, padding the ugly holes on both sides of Foulard's arm with wads of the shirt he'd ripped in small pieces. He finally bound the arm, using the rest of the shirt.

When it was done he told Foulard to take it easy while he rounded up the animals. The black gelding, the pack mule and Indian pony had fled when the shooting started.

Kane climbed up the steep path toward the church to get a look at the country. He tramped toward the far side of the mesa and stopped still. Father Caldero was lying against the church door and his round-crowned wide-brimmed black hat had fallen off. He was beginning to go bald, Kane noted, as he knelt beside the priest and felt for a pulse. Father Caldero was dead, from either a lance thrust or a wound made by a knife in his chest.

Shocked by the padre's death, Kane realized that the Apache's attack had begun in earnest. He wondered about the camp below and about Maurine's safety. He left the mesa quickly to find the horses.

When he came back to camp leading the black, he found Foulard smiling triumphantly. Foulard looked at him with a tight smile and then pointed. Kane followed the direction in which Foulard pointed.

Katterman's wagon moved across the open bench, heading west toward the mountain pass leading to Prescott.

"You ain't gonna have to mind now about Katterman," he said. "He's done got an early start."

CHAPTER 15

Dawn was past. Over the mountains he could see the sun as it edged over the horizon, bright as a gold coin outlining the ragged edges. In the distance a hawk screeched, to be answered by a robber jay lower down. Kane, scanning the area up the creek, noted that three wagons had pulled out into the open and placed to form a triangle around Maurine's tent. Around the important personages, he thought. He wondered what the hell General Crook was thinking about at this moment.

As Kane watched, he saw smoke blossom from the rocks above the wagon, between the camp and the Ghost People ruins. There was answering fire from the wagons. He could see that nothing had happened from the fire. A testing, he surmised.

The sun edged up higher, a blazing ball. It would be a hot day. He could not do much to help Maurine by standing here. He might possibly get one or two Apaches before he went down. Getting himself killed wouldn't solve any problems. He had to get to the wagons, somehow or other.

The Apaches, as was their custom, had dismounted to fight. Nantana fought the Apache way, getting off his horse, which lifted a man to make him a better target. The Indians moved like the wind, becoming one with the rugged terrain. Their horses, Kane decided, were probably in some canyon or arroyo nearby in the care of a horse holder, usually a young man about to become a full-fledged warrior.

Kane went to the black and mounted and put the horse down the creek. He turned upstream, his rifle ready. He reached the still pool where he'd first met Maurine, and for a moment he remembered that time and his feelings then. He touched his heels to the black and splashed across the creek. From somewhere off to the right a shot sounded and he heard the bullet passing, or imagined he did. At the same time a rifle ahead of him opened fire but he couldn't tell if it came from the wagons or from the Apaches.

On the camp side of the creek, he had the black in a dead run now, leaning over the straining horse's neck, firing his rifle with one hand. There was an opening between the wagons ahead of him, an opening about four feet wide, and he put the black directly at this opening, leaping the horse over the wagon tongue and landing inside the enclosure in a cloud of dust, the black squealing with fear.

Kane leaped off the horse, seeing at a glance that Hugh Giles was lying belly-down behind a wagon wheel, firming an army issue Spencer. On the opposite side, Prince Luis coolly fired the handsome hunting rifle but Kane saw no targets.

"Quit shooting at nothing," he said, reloading his rifle as Maurine came from her tent and ran to him, leaning against him, her fright evident. Prince Luis glowered.

"Are you all right?" was her first question.

"Hell—excuse me. I think so. How about you?"

She straightened her face, losing the frightened look. She nodded. "I am—now."

"Professor Flannery has been shot but is alive. Jeffrey, the cook, a nice man, died up there." She pointed to where Kane observed Jeffrey standing guard the day before.

Kane saw Laxton then, at the third wagon. The teamster rolled over and sat up, looking with hatred at Kane, fingering his ruined nose.

She answered the unspoken question in Kane's eyes. "Henry and his men, the civilian employees, were all killed," she said in a shaky voice. "Laxton escaped somehow and came back here to warn us."

"Where's the professor?"

"In my tent. Betty Canfield is taking care of him."

The land was quiet. An occasional gust of wind rustled the canvas of the wagons. The sun beat down, the day heating up. Somewhere in the distance a hawk called shrilly . . . or was it an Apache? They were out there, somewhere, waiting for the right sign, the right time. Kane was sure of it.

Kane went to where Prince Luis was polishing the mechanism of his rifle. The prince wore his blue and gold medallion, the family coat of arms.

"This is not a good place to make a stand," Kane explained. "I think we should fort up in the church. If we can make it there."

"I haven't sighted any of the savages yet," Prince Luis said scornfully. "Are they out there?"

"Yes. If you couldn't see what were you shooting at, why were you firing?"

Prince Luis shrugged. "I fired at the smoke. The others were shooting." He studied Kane. "I have seen no horses. I thought they'd ride in, shooting and screaming."

"Sometimes. They're a very tough people, Prince. The Apache don't depend on the horse in the way, say, the Comanches or the Plains Indians do. First you see them, then you don't. They ride when it's advantageous. They can melt into the ground right before your eyes. They can appear the same way. They're probably the roughest fighting people in the world."

Prince Luis gave his rifle one last wipe of the cloth and laid it aside. "You think we should make a dash for the church?"

"Yes. The priest is dead. The Apaches killed him."

Prince Luis' face expressed shock but after a silence he crossed himself and said, "These murderous savages will pay for that."

"If we're not careful—and lucky, very lucky—those murderous savages as you call them will exact payment from us. They have means of torture that can send a man stark raving mad with pain."

Prince Luis looked at the ground between his legs. "I'd like to meet one face to face."

"You're not likely to," Kane replied, "until you're breathing your last breath."

The prince was silent and Kane went on, "I'll check and see if Flannery can be moved." He nodded to the prince and walked toward Maurine's tent.

He called out and then entered the tent. Flannery lay on Maurine's bed and Betty sat on a camp stool beside the bed, holding Flannery's hand.

Flannery turned his head as Kane stood at the foot of the bed.

"The worst has happened, Kane," he said weakly. "I'm out of brandy." He tried to smile.

Betty patted his hand.

"I want to know if you can make it to the church," Kane said grimly. "We'll be safer there. The church is much more defensible than this open space."

Flannery nodded. "We—we didn't pick this place for its defense potential," he said. "I took a bullet through my right side. I think it nicked a lung but I'll make it. I've got to make it because Porter Canfield made some important discoveries here and they must be made public. Betty and I will work on it together, prepare a paper . . ." His voice trailed away, he muttered incoherently and lapsed into unconsciousness.

"He is delirious sometimes," Betty said with her lips pursed. "Porter made no startling discovery here, Mr. Kane. He simply enjoyed poking around in the ruins and speculating on the origin of Egyptian and Hebrew influence but nothing conclusive."

"Can we move Flannery?"

"I don't think so. He's bleeding internally and is very weak."

"We can't get a wagon to the church. Too steep going up the mesa. But we may put him on a horse."

She was shaking her head as he talked. "He's too weak to stay on a horse."

"A travois maybe," Kane said. "We'll see what can be done. If the Apaches rush this place we may all end up in worse shape than Flannery."

She shivered and rounded her shoulders defensively.

He turned silently and left the tent. Hugh Giles was standing outside, waiting.

Kane stopped short, alert, ready for anything.

Giles stared at him, hard-eyed. "You got it out, didn't you?" he asked, low-voiced. "I'm talkin' about the gold, Kane."

"That's not any of your business," Kane said coldly.

"Maybe it is. Maybe not. Where's Foulard?"

"Foulard's holed up in the church."

"A likely story. You probably killed him so you can have it all for yourself."

"Think what you will. It matters little to me."

The two men faced each other in the bright morning sun, hovering on the edge of violence.

"Stop it!" Prince Luis barked with his rifle leveled at the space between the two of them. "First one of you who makes a move to his gun I'll kill. We've got those murderous savages to fight. We need every gun."

Kane turned away and went to the supply wagon and began looking for material to make a travois. He found two spare tent poles and laid them out side by side. He climbed up on the wagon and began ripping off the canvas cover to make a sling to carry Flannery to the church, and saw that some of the villagers had gathered on the mesa.

They found Father Caldero's body. These village women were familiar with death. They would know what to do.

Kane went on with his work. The sun came higher, bringing more heat. The land was quiet. Nothing moved except an occasional hawk high in the sky. The wind rustled the canvas and now and then a mule squalled from the rope corral.

It took Kane almost an hour to get the travois ready. When it was done he fastened it to a pack mule from the army remuda. He motioned Giles and Laxton to help him and they brought Flannery from the tent and placed him on the travois. His white shirt was stained with blood.

"If they jump us it'll be when we move away from the wagons," said Kane tersely. "You, Giles, and Prince Luis swing out on either side. Laxton walks drag. Fire at anything that moves. The women will walk between the pack mules."

"Yes, *sir*," Giles said sarcastically, touching his hand to his hat brim. He'd been outfitted in army clothing and was hardly recognizable as the scarecrow who had straggled into camp a day or so ago.

Prince Luis simply looked at Giles with disgust and walked away.

The procession set out, heading down the creek on the trail leading to the church. Kane had put a long lead on the pack mule pulling the travois, and he was out in front, holding his Winchester in his right hand, ready to fire at anything moving.

They had traveled five minutes when Kane looked back. The wagons were in flames but he still couldn't see a single Apache. Kane felt a surge of relief as the train got through the first thick growth and the trees began thinning out. The church loomed ahead like some beacon, a symbol of safety. Suddenly a figure appeared on the mesa beside the church, running past the church and down the incline with the grace of a deer.

"Don't shoot!" Kane shouted. "That's Juanita!"

He shouted for her to go back but she kept coming. An Apache seemed to erupt from the ground, moving to intercept her. Kane dropped the lead rope and threw the rifle to his shoulder, aiming for a body shot. He squeezed the trigger and the brown body tumbled down the slope until a rock stopped the tumble. He struggled for a moment and then slumped back, losing hold on his lance, which rolled out of sight.

Not faltering, Juanita ran on. She was carrying a small bundle which she hung on to. She dodged through the trees, jumped the narrow part of the creek and turned upstream, running into Kane with a force that shook him and clinging to him.

She panted for a moment, looked up at him, lifting the

small bundle. "This is all I own," she said. "You are leaving. I go with you."

Kane was still holding her. He stepped away, glancing over his shoulder. Maurine was staring off into the distance.

"We're not leaving," Kane said. "We're trying to reach the church where we can fight the Apache."

Before she could reply a shot sounded. Prince Luis had dropped an Apache on the incline above and he was aiming for another. The Apache vanished before Luis got off his second shot.

"Come on, let's move it!" Kane shouted and picked up the lead rope again and pulled the mule into motion.

They went down the creek, Kane trotting now, jerking at the lead rope. He looked back and saw Prince Luis still standing, looking for the elusive Apache.

"Luis! Come on!" Kane bawled.

Prince Luis reluctantly followed. He and Giles came together at the ford, where the trail crossed the creek, and Kane kept looking back as the main party climbed the incline to the mesa.

Kane had almost reached the lip of the mesa when firing began. A shot rang out and Kane fired almost as the muzzle flame stabbed from a tree. An Apache lunged out from behind the tree, stumbled and regained his footing, shooting, and Kane and Prince Luis fired at the same time, knocking him to the ground.

Running hard, Kane reached the lip of the mesa and, turning, blasted two shots in the direction of the firing.

Juanita took up the lead rope and tugged the mule over the rim, in toward the church. Prince Luis, Giles and Laxton came up the incline, turning to fire as they went.

Kane watched them gain the mesa and he turned, loading his rifle at the same time. Juanita had the mule at the church door and stood there, waiting. Kane and Giles carried the wounded man inside. Maurine had a dazed look in her eyes as she followed. Betty was crying quietly, as she walked beside Flannery, holding his hand.

There were a dozen women and even more children in one corner of the church. They looked at him in stony silence, almost accusingly, Kane thought.

All of them were inside now, standing quietly, looking at one another. Betty Canfield knelt beside Flannery's litter, wiping his brow, chafing his hands.

Giles was standing there staring up at Jesus on the cross, over the altar. He looked around and said, "What the hell now?"

"Let's get a lookout up in the bell tower," Kane said. He spoke to Juanita. "Show me the way up."

She silently led him into the vestibule. His shoulder brushed the pull rope to the bells above. She entered a small trap door and pointed up. Luis started to follow but Giles stepped in front of him.

"I'll go," he said and followed Kane up the steep ladder leading to the tower.

Kane emerged onto the platform below the bells. He bumped against one of the bells and a hollow sound seemed to make the entire church vibrate.

The entire countryside was visible from the tower, through the arches. The village lay in the westering sun, dead and lifeless. It seemed that even the goats, pigs, sheep and chickens had taken cover.

The mountain crest to the east was bathed in light from the swiftly sinking sun on the western horizon. In all the expanse of land around the mesa nothing moved within his sight, except a lone hawk winging toward the mountains, a dust devil here and there. He felt no wind on his face.

Giles stood at Kane's back. "I found your tunnel," he said. "I know you got the gold out, Kane. I want it."

"The gold is not yours, Giles. Don't make the mistake of trying to take it."

"What've you done with it?" Giles asked in a rough voice. "I know you have it. See here!" He thrust a gold bar before Kane's eyes. "Pure gold, for real. Now where's the rest of it?"

Kane studied the gold bar, remembering how he'd dropped it on the ground just before the Apache attack. What Giles didn't know was that he'd brought out only one bar. Maybe the tunnel had caved in again, preventing him from entering the underground chamber. "Forget it, Giles," Kane advised. "It won't get you nothing but trouble."

Giles's face twisted with frustration and rage and he visibly fought it down. He jammed the gold bar back into his military pouch and fastened the snap.

"Keep your eyes open," Kane said, moving toward the ladder leading to the church below. "I'll see you get spelled in an hour or so."

Giles grunted as Kane went down the ladder. Maurine waited in the vestibule. She leaned against the wall, brushing her hair back as she silently watched him take the last few rungs of the ladder. He stood his rifle against the wall.

"She won, didn't she?" Maurine asked softly, looking at him wide-eyed. "We could have had so much fun together."

"You distress me."

"It is Juanita, isn't it? I saw her, bringing her pitiful lit-

tle bundle of belongings, begging you to take her away."
She grasped his arm. "Jared, don't throw yourself away on
someone you'll tire of in no time at all. You have nothing
in common."

He wrinkled his forehead in a forbidding frown but she
rushed on: "My father is a very important man in the
U. S. Government. Mr. Hayes trusts him. Mr. Hayes
doesn't get along with Congress and may not run for
office again. My father could very well be the next Presi-
dent."

"I'm sure he'd deserve it," Kane said.

"Oh, damn!" she said and fled.

CHAPTER 16

After full dark Kane sent Laxton to the bell tower to relieve Giles. When Giles came into the vestibule, Señor Gonzales and his two sons entered through the big door.

"Where the hell them greasers been?" he demanded. He strode over to confront Gonzales. "Been out there hobnobbin' with them 'Paches, I bet." He eyed Kane rancorously. "Wanna bet?"

"They don't understand you," said Kane. "Not one of them understands English."

"Well, what the hell." Giles broke into badly broken Spanish, demanding to know where the three had been, if they were talking to the Apaches.

Gonzales drew himself up, pulled his coat together and opened with a torrent of Spanish.

"Hey, damn, don't talk so fast," ordered Giles.

"What he said was he's the chief of his village," Kane interpreted, "and that if you insult him again he may have you hanged." Kane added, "If he needs help doing it, I'll give him a hand, Giles." He went to the door, opened it, looked out and then stepped through, carrying his Winchester in his right hand. The air was still, as though a storm was coming, though the sky was clear except for a few dying cumulus over the mountains.

He took a slow walk around the rim of the mesa, stopping above where his and Foulard's camp had been. The Apache he'd shot there was gone. They retrieve their dead, he thought somberly, and walked on, surveying the land in all directions. He stopped, studying the area from where the Summers' party had camped all the way down to the ford. A blackened area, littered with the iron work and iron rims of the wheels, marked where the wagons had been standing.

Kane shifted his position, moving along the edge of the mesa. When he found a shallow break in the rim, he settled down into it to watch and wait.

Nothing happened. The sun was nearly on the western horizon but sending down heat. A vinegarroon scuttled across his moccasined foot and he kicked instinctively, throwing the insect against a rock. It scurried away, its venomous tail raised. Down in the trees along the creek a jay squawked noisily. The land was empty, desert and mountains still as death itself.

Kane wiped his forehead with his sleeve. The slash across his chest from the Apache knife itched and he guessed that meant it was healing.

Only Kane knew the predicament all of them were in. He'd found to his dismay that the roof of the church wouldn't support the weight of an average-sized man. They would not be able to fight off an attack from the roof and the bell tower was not large enough for two men. Maybe he'd led all of them into a death trap.

He thought about what could be done as he searched the terrain, working slowly from right to left and back again. He glanced over his shoulder and saw Luis in the bell tower. The Spanish prince had a pair of binoculars and was scanning the same area as Kane.

Kane frowned. He'd sent Laxton to the tower. Luis was looking for action. That could mean more trouble.

He got to his feet and continued to circle the mesa until he was back where he'd started. He stood there for a long moment and then went inside the church as the sun dipped below the western horizon, seeming to drop all at once.

It's going to be a long night, he thought.

Laxton was talking to one of the villagers and Kane motioned him over. "I sent you up to the tower to take guard," Kane said.

"Well, this prince feller said he'd take it," Laxton said defensively. "He told me it'd be all right."

"It's not all right," said Kane. "Get on up there and send him down."

Kane cleaned his pistol and was starting on his rifle when Prince Luis came from the tower. He went directly to the door and opened it.

"Where you going, Luis?" Kane called.

Prince Luis patted his rifle. "To look about and see if I may bag another Apache."

"You'd best not go out there right now."

"I'll find a hidden place and wait for one," he said. "Lugo showed me how to hunt deer that way."

"Lugo's dead," Kane said. "You won't find an Apache like that, but one is likely to find you. And cut your throat. Close the door."

Prince Luis hesitated and then closed the door. He came to stand beside Kane. "I know there must always be someone in charge," he said. "But must it be you?"

"Maybe we'll match for it," Kane said dryly.

"Match? What is this match?"

"We toss a coin and you call it. If you call it right you may be in charge."

Prince Luis frowned. "You joke with me," he said and strode across the room to where Maurine sat beside Flannery. He said something to her in a low voice and she looked at Kane without smiling.

Juanita brought Kane a bowl of beans and tortillas and he sat against the wall eating, breaking off pieces of the tortilla and using it to spoon spicy red beans into his mouth. Knives, forks and spoons were unknown even in the homes of Armijo. He remembered the small joke Maurine had made about the lack of silverware at the Katterman party.

Foulard still sat in a dark corner, where he'd been since all of them had taken cover in the church. He was being fed by a handsome older Mexican woman called Luz. He seemed to be in some pain but the liberal application of brandy seemed to have prevented infection.

Kane had not taken a survey of food and water available—he'd not had time for that. But it was something he must do and then set up a rationing system, if necessary. And it would be necessary, he thought grimly, if Nantana hung on, and there was no reason to believe the Apache leader wouldn't do just that. A lot of personal prestige and, more importantly, additional warriors joining him, hung in balance.

After eating, Kane assigned watches during the night to Prince Luis and Giles and then climbed the tower to allow Laxton time off.

Laxton was reluctant to leave. "You think we can get out o' this?"

"I'd say about fifty-fifty," Kane said, "if our food and water hold out."

"I'd say we ought t' try an' sneak outa here and make it to the fort."

"There's the women and children for me to think about."

"You mean all them greasers—"

"Shut up, Laxton," Kane said shortly. "I don't want to listen to that kind of talk."

"Well, that's your worry," Laxton said and went through the trap door.

Kane sat there in the darkness and all the land was dark, seeming to accentuate the brightness of the stars in the sky. A thin sliver of moon edged over the mountain, softening the rugged terrain. He sat still, hearing the murmur of voices from below, strained and stifled, betraying the fear that haunted the church. He sat still, trying to shut out the voices below and listen only to the night sounds. He was aware of a presence and Juanita slipped in and sat close to him, her arm touching his arm as they silently watched the stars. It seemed to bring them closer together.

But there were other things. "Your father and brothers, where were they?" he asked. "They came after all the others had gathered in the church."

She grasped his arm. "My father is the chief," she said simply. "He had to be sure the old and the sick were not left behind. It is his duty."

Kane felt a moment of shame.

"You are angry with me?"

"No, not angry, Juanita. I couldn't be angry with you."

"Then I may go with you?"

"You're excited and scared," he said softly. "That makes you turn to me, anyone. Think about it, Juanita."

"I've thought of it, Jared Kane. I've thought of nothing else for so long, since I first saw you and knew you had come for me."

He felt an ache somewhere in the region of his heart. He had nothing more to say. He thought of Maurine Summers and the ache deepened. Maurine was a completely self-sufficient woman. Juanita felt she needed him. He was torn by conflicting emotions he couldn't readily understand.

"Your father would not look kindly on this, Juanita."

"My father thinks all Americans are Yankees. He does not trust. But you, he likes. He say you are honest and strong. And he think you better than most gringo."

Kane chuckled. "I'm no different from the rest of them."

Her fingers tightened on his arm. "To me you are mos' different," she said. "I look at you and I know you can do anything, anything at all, Jared Kane."

"If we can get out of this I'll be satisfied," he said and she sighed and laid her head against his shoulder.

Afterward she went below to sleep and Kane continued to watch, though he felt there was little chance the Apache would move at night.

In the sky the stars changed. In the far distance he heard the lonely howl of a coyote yearning for a mate. There was no rest for him as he mulled over the situation. Yet he was not excited, not even worried. His years had let him see that each predicament was to be met as it neared, and nothing much could be done until it came time to act. Right now there was only the waiting.

Kane had no fear of Nantana. He'd had brushes with Indians much of his life and felt he knew them as well as anyone. A more immediate danger was Giles, unpredictable, dangerous, perhaps unstable. The man had come through a bad time. Kane didn't know the truth of the relationship between Giles and Foulard and he thought perhaps he'd never know. His only real conviction was that he had to watch Giles. And maybe Laxton. The teamster had not forgotten the savage beating Kane had administered when he'd tried to rape the Mexican woman. . . . Kane sighed heavily. A man did what he had to do. That was as near as he could come to voicing his personal feeling and belief.

Considering Nantana, Kane did not think of him as a good or bad Indian. The Apache, as with other tribes, had suffered fearfully at the hands of the white man. In a way, Kane sympathized with Nantana, in what seemed to him a last-ditch fight against encroachment on his land, culture and religion, and in fact his life and that of his people. So he killed people with no more thought of it than slapping a mosquito? War had always been an occupation, avocation and obsession with Apaches, as well as other warlike tribes. It was the tradition in which he had been born and it was one in which he would die. In that same light, Kane had felt the weight of injustice and even heartache. He'd not let it draw him into the violence that tempted him from time to time. Each man made his own decisions and lived by them if he was all man.

Prince Luis climbed into the tower rubbing his eyes sleepily. "I am not sleep so well," he said. "Only when it is ready to stand guard do I feel sleepy."

Kane felt little inclination to make conversation with the prince. He said, "So long, Luis. Keep awake."

After a long night and daylight, Kane went to the bell tower to allow Giles to take a break.

Sleepy-eyed and grouchy, Giles muttered, "Ain't seen hide'r hair o' man or beast." He squeezed by Kane and stood in the opening. "You think them Apaches pulled out?"

Kane pointed instead of answering. A lone Apache on a spotted pony came down the rough terrain near the cliff-house ruins, his horse running hard, seeming to flow downward, a picture of grace and movement. He was beyond the range of even a buffalo gun. "There goes one of his scouts."

Giles nodded, growling, "Goddamn savage sonofabitches, I wisht he was in range."

Kane straightened, suddenly fully alert, his heart pounding. Prince Luis appeared on the mesa below them and began descending from the tiny island on the vast slope that rose gradually from the village of Armijo in the flatland to the base of the mountains. "What the hell is he up to?"

"He's always gabblin' about gettin' himself an Apache," Giles said. "Maybe he's goin' down there to bag one."

"He'll get himself killed," Kane said. He yelled at Luis but the prince didn't give any indication that he had heard. "Stay here, Giles, and watch while I go after him."

"I'll do that for you, Kane," Giles said agreeably. He laid his rifle across the base of an arch and said softly, "Looks like the 'Paches are gonna save me the trouble of killin' you, Kane. Here they come!"

The haul from the wagon train of the Summers' party had been disappointing to Nantana. In addition, earlier in the morning he'd lost his friend of a lifetime, Talin, the warrior he trusted most of all.

He had to be alone to try to talk to those of the spirit world who might be inclined to help him.

Nantana ran lithely, bent-kneed, with his back straight as he'd run all his life. He had not been softened by easy living and he was proud that he could outdistance and outlast his youngest and strongest brave.

His spirits were not high and he ran to recapture a spirit greater than himself that he felt was near. He grieved for Talin, the sly and cunning one who'd died at the hands of the tall gold-haired man.

Reaching the lonely heights above the ruins of the Ghost People, Nantana stood on a promontory and sought the feeling he experienced when trying to talk to those who favored him in the spirit world. He began communing only after properly scanning the area for lurking enemies.

The Apache were never safe, not in their own lands. They could cook mescal only when they felt safe and those places of safety were few and far between. The Apache were hated by Mexicans, Americans, and all the other tribes. One of the names bestowed upon the Apache by the Navajo was—the Enemy.

As he stood there, his face lifted to the sky, he chanted the old Apache way, calling on the Earth Mother, Father Sun and all the Brothers of the animal world to succor him in his hour of anguish for a lost friend and ally— brave and faithful Talin. He felt a bitter hatred creep into him for the gold-haired one called Kane, and he resisted that hate because he'd found that such a feeling destroyed his ability to communicate with the universe as he coaxed the spirits out to aid him, advise him and to give him cunning and strength.

After his meditation he had a good feeling and he walked erect and with great strides back to where his braves were camped, just below where the Summers' wagons had been burned.

They'd not realized much from that raid and he was disappointed. Talin had told him of the guns, lead, powder and other valuables the crazy white-eyes had cached in their wagons.

It is not Talin's fault, he thought defensively. It is the crazy white-eyes who will do anything. Momentarily, Nantana wished for a young, very young, man to be with him, as sometimes these young ones had visions that were sacred.

There were now thirty warriors in Nantana's band. He needed more. To get more he had to win here at Armijo.

The day was late and the warriors lay around talking,

taking care of their weapons and their horses and examining some of the loot they'd taken from the Summers' wagon train. One item, a picture of a man in a strange uniform with many medals, caused some excitement. Taking the picture, Nantana recognized the man described by Talin as the one who resembled him. The Apache leader made no mention of this to the others and he assumed his braves did not notice the resemblance.

He threw the picture in the fire. "Bad medicine," he said.

Cashis, the shaman, sought Nantana out and called him aside, after motioning a Coyotero Apache to accompany them. The brave was a recent recruit from across the mountain.

"This man comes from the army place," Cashis said. "He has looked with his own eyes on what the horse soldiers are up to. Listen to him, Nantana."

"I listen," Nantana said.

The short, stocky Apache was articulate and had keen and observant eyes. The leader of the horse soldiers was a strange one, a man who dressed, not in army uniform, but in the clothes of the white-eyes. This General Crook rode a mule and carried a double-barreled shotgun and at times he went away from his troops alone, except for an Indian guide, and maybe one horse soldier. There were as many horse soldiers as the mountains held rocks, they had many mules to carry supplies, for pack mules were faster than wagons. Even now, a large column of horse soldiers was circling the territory.

With a stick the Coyotero traced out the route thus far of a large body of cavalry. He threw the stick away and stood upright.

"That's the way it is," he said.

Cashis waved him away. "You do not have enough braves to fight such a force," Cashis said.

Nantana's nostrils flared and his eyes grew fierce. He waved his hand toward the church. "When I have taken those up there, more warriors will come."

"You have the best of them now," Cashis said. "Geronimo is looking for brave warriors too."

"You were supposed to make medicine for me, shaman," Nantana complained. "Why have you not done so?"

"That I will in due course," Cashis said. "I will bring you victory after victory. All the tribes will hear of your feats and good men will join you."

"Then I wait no longer," Nantana said. "We will go up there and kill them all this very day."

CHAPTER 17

Kane shoved his rifle through the arch and fired with one hand as the first brown body emerged from cover at the base of the mesa. The Apaches came from all sides.

"Do what you can!" Kane said, "I'll try to get Prince Luis back inside before he loses his hair."

He went down the ladder, taking several rungs at a time. Going through the big door, he motioned Foulard to close it behind him.

He circled the church and approached the rim, firing at flitting, darting figures, trying to drive them back yet conserving ammunition.

Kane had a glimpse of Ramon and Felipe sending fire down into the Apaches from the west windows. By God, he thought exultantly, Juanita is loading for them. Then he was down in the black rocks, yelling at Luis to turn back.

He had a quick look at Giles in the bell tower, shooting down over his head. He imagined he could hear the whir of the leaden pellets and flinched at the thought of being under Giles's gun.

Prince Luis turned, with a puzzled frown on his face, and then as quickly as it had started, the firing stopped. The Apaches simply disappeared except for the lone figure of Nantana, standing erect, his black, shoulder-length hair confined in a band of red calico. Naked except for a breechclout and a bandoleer hanging from his shoulder and across his massive chest, he carried no weapon other than the knife at his belt.

The two men stared at one another, the Spanish prince and the Apache leader, and then Nantana vanished.

Luis came back toward Kane. "Mother of Jesus! Did you see what that savage was wearing?"

Kane grasped the prince's arm and gave him a shove up toward the church. "You're putting us all in danger!" Kane said roughly. "Get the hell back inside and don't try anything like that again."

Prince Luis thrust out the blue and gold medallion hanging from his neck. "That beastly savage wore a medallion exactly as this one—my family's coat of arms, for more than three centuries!"

Kane gave Prince Luis a final shove into the church vestibule when Foulard cautiously opened the door. "I'm not interested in medals," Kane said. "I'm more concerned with keeping us all alive—for as long as possible."

Prince Luis hastened across the room to squat beside Flannery. "I can't understand it," he said, as he described his brief meeting with Nantana.

Flannery sat up, coughing, and blood appeared on his lips. "Where's my pencil? Where's my notebook? Give them to me so I can put this down."

"He's delirious again," Betty Canfield whispered tearfully.

"No! No, I'm not. Don't you see, Luis? This man is perhaps a relative of yours. He's a distant cousin, no doubt, from your great-grandmother, who was carried away by the Apache at Vidalpando!"

"Impossible," Prince Luis muttered. "For me, of the royal blood of Spain to be related to that murderous savage."

Flannery lay back. "They came across the bridge," he

murmured, "the Apache, maybe two thousand, three thousand years ago, hungry and tough, hated by every being they met, driven from Canada, driven from the Great Plains, they finally made a stand in this savage country. . . ."

Prince Luis rose and stood looking down at Flannery and then leaned his rifle against the wall and crossed the room to where the Mexican women from the village clustered with their children.

Gonzales had somehow managed to get his bull-hide chair into the church and slumbered in it with his hat pulled down over his face.

Ramon and Felipe manned the two windows on the west side, while Laxton paced from one window to the other on the east. Foulard had resumed his place in a dark corner where he sat huddled with his arms clasped around his legs, his head resting on his knees.

Maurine Summers and Betty Canfield sat on each side of Flannery, who was again unconscious but muttering incoherently.

Prince Luis appeared to be dickering with one of the Mexican women. He gave her gold coins and then hoisted an earthenware jug to his shoulder and headed toward the back of the church, toward the priest's quarters.

"Where you going with that water?" Kane asked.

Prince Luis stopped. "For a bath, of course."

"We need all the water for drinking purposes," Kane said. "None for bathing."

"How absurd!" exclaimed Prince Luis and continued on his way.

Kane stepped ahead of him, facing him. "You don't seem to realize the danger of our situation," Kane said patiently, struggling to keep his voice and anger down.

"Maybe Nantana and his warriors can't get in but we can't get out. We'll have to ration the food and water."

"We have plenty," Prince Luis said impatiently.

Their argument, soft though it was, had attracted the attention of those in the church.

Gonzales awoke, pushed up his hat, rose and came to them in his role of chief of the village.

"What is this?" he demanded. "Why do you quarrel when the enemy is at our door?"

"We must conserve water and Prince Luis wants to take a bath," Kane said, irritated that he had to do this out of dire necessity.

"It is better to have a hen tomorrow than an egg today," Gonzales said. "Forget this bath, Luis, until we are rid of the Apache."

"Your Spanish is terrible," Luis said, "but your words are those of a wise man." He returned the water to the Mexican woman and refused to accept the coins she offered him.

Kane made a swift survey of food and water, including an inventory of the priest's quarters. He found the small, square room, with a single window looking out on the mountains, quite austere. There was a narrow bed, a table containing a Bible, and another small table holding papers and two dried, wrinkled apples.

The kitchen yielded little more—a small bag of corn meal and a jug of water. He took these back into the church and put them with the other foodstuff he'd collected.

Not more than enough for two days, three at the most. He shook his head. It was the lack of water that concerned him. One could endure without food for weeks. Without water, one died quickly—and horribly.

Gonzales said, "That is all there is?"

Kane nodded. "Not enough, sir, for more than two days."

"Ah, me," Gonzales said. "I will keep watch on it, my son, and see that all share alike."

Kane agreed with a nod and climbed the ladder to the bell tower. He scanned the hot countryside in all directions and then settled down to wait.

Nothing moved. The sun beat down on the sloping bench that rose steadily but not steeply from the village to the base of the mountains. A bee flew in and out of the bell tower with a buzzing, angry sound. A bird lit on the edge of the church roof, teetering there for a moment before flying away in a swift flash of color. The sky was deep blue and as silent as the mountains and desert.

The Apaches were out there, waiting.

Kane didn't know if Nantana had lost warriors in the latest fire fight but it seemed the numbers had increased. Kane knew well enough that the odds were against them. The Apaches were perhaps the world's greatest guerrilla fighters.

A slow hour passed. All was stillness. He searched the terrain and thought he detected movement in the willows along the creek. He worked his eyes back and forth along the creek, and on down to where the diversion ditch began. He caught sight of a bobbing movement, and tensed for a moment before deciding it was a quail.

The sun declined a little, the shadows growing longer. The wind rose, bringing puffs of dust out on the bench and moving the cottonwoods and willows along the creek.

He got to his knees as Juanita came through the opening with beans on a plate and the canteen. He ate quickly while she watched. He took a sparing gulp from the canteen to wash down the fiery frijoles.

"You are all right, no?"

He chuckled. "I'm all right, yes," he said. "What about you?"

An evening breeze, cooling, moved through the arches as they watched together the benchland beneath them and there was nothing in sight. They looked at each other and smiled.

"You are like the desert and mountains," she said suddenly. "Always there, always the same, strong and steady . . ."

The last gold was fading from the distant sky. The long loom of the land in the far west darkened and the shadows crept up the face of the near mountains. He checked his rifle again.

Somewhere a night bird called and was answered from afar.

"What shall we do, Jared?"

He shook his head and then realized it was too dark for her to see the motion. "About Nantana? Or about the men here inside the church who would like to see me dead?"

She impulsively grasped his arm. "I will watch for you. I will warn you if anyone threatens . . ."

He chuckled. "I knew I could depend on you. I'm safe so long as Nantana hangs on." He was silent for a long time and then he said, "There's an underground chamber beneath the church, Juanita. Yes, and a tunnel that leads outside. The stairway to the underground chamber is directly in front of the altar."

"How is it you know this, Jared?"

"I tunneled in beneath the church and found it."

"You were looking for gold, no?"

"Yes, I was looking for gold. I came to Armijo to look for gold."

It took him a while to realize that she was crying quietly, without sound. He pulled her to him and smoothed her hair and awkwardly patted her shoulder. She relaxed in his arms and gradually quieted.

"I do not know why I do that, cry," she said. "My father say you look for gold and I tell him no, no, no!"

"I was looking for more than gold when I came here," Kane said softly. "I didn't know it then but I know it now."

He rose to his feet and lifted her. She leaned against him for a moment and he felt her shiver as a sound invaded the tower. A swishing sound. Then silence.

He cocked his ear to the night and heard nothing. Then the noise started, a gentle grating sound as though something, a branch of a tree, moved back and forth. He leaned over the edge of the arch and could see nothing. He went to another arch, the one looking over the roof to the south. He could see the seesaw motion of something down there. He slipped over the edge of the arch and hung to the ledge until his feet found a solid beam to stand on. He let go and squatted there, looking at what was the Apache version of a file or saw, a thin line of knotted rawhide, sliding back and forth, cutting into the adobe of which the tower was constructed. He'd seen native workmen use the knotted rawhide to cut openings for windows and doors in adobe construction. He realized the sound he'd heard was an arrow to which the rawhide was attached. He drew his knife and slashed the rawhide, the ends flying off into the night.

He looked up to see Juanita's face wreathed in anxiety.

"It's all right," he said. "I'll be right up." He walked the beam to the front and looked down into darkness but could see nothing in the total darkness. Nantana had braves at his disposal who did not fear the night. That makes me uneasy, he thought, as he climbed back into the bell tower.

"It's time to make a move," he said. "Let's go below."

CHAPTER 18

The candlelight made grotesque shadows on the wall of the church as Kane and Laxton stood before the altar. Juanita lighted another candle to give better light. Kane got down on his hands and knees, tapping on the floor with the butt of his Colt. In less than five minutes he had outlined the trap door.

Whatever had to be done must be done quickly. Kane hoped to be out of the church and on his way for help in the darkest part of the night, just before dawn. He hoped against hope that the black gelding had not been taken by the Apaches.

"Search through the church," Kane directed Laxton. "See what tools you can find." He had small hope there'd be anything useful because Father Caldero had been unable to furnish the simple tools needed to repair the church. It seemed a hundred years ago that he'd handled the rough stones in rebuilding the corner that had fallen in.

Kane began digging with his knife and found immediately that the floor surface, made of clay, locally called caliche, mixed with ox blood, was like solid rock. He broke his knife blade in less than a minute or two.

Laxton returned with a foot-long chisel and a small hand sledge. "Found these in a little shop off the padre's room," he said.

When Kane began pounding on the floor with the chisel and hammer it awoke all in the church. A child cried in the darkness and its mother talked soothingly. Juanita went to help quiet the child. Maurine wrinkled her forehead, her mouth drooping, shaking her head in annoyance.

Old Gonzales came out of the shadows and squatted on the floor, his elbows on his knees, cupping his jaws with his hands.

"When you get out, the Apache will be waiting," Gonzales said. "Like the wolf waiting at a rabbit hole. The Apache, they are good at waiting."

Kane kept pounding away with the hammer and chisel. Dust drifted up into his face. He snagged his neckerchief over his nose and continued working. Sweat dribbled down on the dark-red clay, turning crimson.

"Let me," Laxton said and took the hammer from Kane and continued the work.

Once loosened, the crusted clay covering came up in chunks that could be lifted out and laid aside. Slowly, the area Kane had indicated was uncovered, revealing the stones.

Stone had simply been laid on top of planks and came out easily. Kane stacked them around the edge of the trap door.

He hurried, trying to beat daylight, using the chisel to pry up the trap door. The rotted leather hinges gave way and he lifted the trap door out and saw the steps leading down into the underground chamber.

He slung a canteen over his shoulder and stepped through the opening.

"Wait," Juanita commanded. "You are the leader here, Jared Kane. You cannot go."

"I don't agree with that," Maurine Summers said coolly, stepping forward. "He's the strongest. He's most likely to get through for help."

Kane looked from one to the other. Then he looked up

in Laxton's face and then Giles's, finally turning his head toward Gonzales, waiting.

"What's it to be?" he asked quietly.

"You must remain here," Gonzales said. "The women and children need you. We all need you, my son."

"Any volunteers?" Kane asked dryly.

Giles's hand shot up. "I learned a few tricks livin' with them red devils," he said. "I reckon I got as good a chance gettin' through as anybody." He gave Kane a hard, level look. "Not exceptin' you, either."

Kane stepped back up into the room. "All right, then," he said, unslinging his canteen and handing it to Giles. "Take a few tortillas. It'll have to do. If you use more than two days getting to Fort Defiance there's going to be some hungry, thirsty people here." He didn't say it but he knew he was speaking of death for them all.

"I'll do the best I know how," Giles said and stepped down through the opening and descended into darkness.

There was a rush to the windows overlooking the campsite where Kane and Foulard had started the tunnel. It was dark out there but maybe, just maybe, Kane thought, they'd be able to knock down any Apache hiding in that area with notions of stopping anyone from escaping. . . .

All the candles had been extinguished. When all the group that could gather around windows were there, Foulard raised his head and looked around, warily. He rose and went swiftly to the trap-door opening, stepped through and descended the stone steps, his moccasined feet making no sound.

Foulard stumbled in the dark but kept going, feeling his way. A match flared and Foulard stopped, watching Giles's face appear as he touched his match to a candle stub. Giles turned and went toward the furnace retort and stuck the candle on the forge. He stood looking at the gold bars and then quickly began shoving the innocuous-appearing bars into his pockets and into the army pouch on his belt.

Giles whirled, his face hard and his eyes cold.

"You rotten, lyin', cheatin' sonofabitch," he said, and drew his pistol and cocked it.

"Go ahead, shoot," taunted Foulard. "That'll bring 'em runnin', bucko."

Giles savagely jammed his pistol back into his holster and, leaning over, snatched a halberd from the floor and buried it in Foulard's chest with one vicious thrust. "That'll fix you, you thievin' bastard," he said, as Foulard gasped, grabbing at the halberd, trying to pull it out.

Blood geysered from around the blade and Foulard dropped to his knees, his eyes walling until only the whites showed. He gasped once and fell backward, his hands clutching the hook of the halberd. He shuddered and lay still.

Giles turned without another glance and continued to fill his pockets with gold bars. When he could find no more space he snuffed out the candle and, slumping under the weight of the gold, made his way to the hole in the wall Kane had told him about. He had some difficulty getting into the tunnel because of his burden. He had no thought of discarding a single bar of gold. He thought, I'll come back for the rest of it when this is all over.

CHAPTER 19

When Kane reached the bell tower Prince Luis moved aside to make room for him in the cramped space. Kane looked down into the darkness and could see nothing. There was no moon and he appreciated it while at the same time wishing for better viewing.

"I have seen nothing," Prince Luis said.

"That doesn't mean a thing. Giles could be long gone by now."

"I pray that is so," murmured Luis, shifting his rifle.

The two of them, Kane and Prince Luis, watched as dawn broke and brightened into full daylight, silent, morose. Nothing moved in the vast expanse of lonely desert, benchland and mountains.

Kane crawled through an arch, onto the ledge of the church proper, and walked along the beam until he could glimpse the small valley where the animals had grazed. The black gelding, the pack mule and Indian pony were not in sight.

That could mean the Indians had taken them, they'd wandered off in search of grass—or Giles had found the black and ridden him away. Kane returned to the bell tower.

Kane watched for another half hour and then left the tower, promising to send Laxton up to relieve Luis.

Prince Luis shook his head. "I'll stay here. I hope for a shot at Nantana."

"Any Apache will do," Kane said dryly.

"I would like to take him alive, take him back to Spain, find out where he got my family medallion—"

"Is a medal so important?"

"To me, yes," Prince Luis said simply. "It is a symbol of my heritage."

Kane smiled faintly. "A heritage you don't wish to share with an Apache?"

Prince Luis nodded, seriously. "Yes, that is part of it—" He stopped speaking and quickly raised his rifle as an Apache appeared at the rim of the mesa. He and Kane fired at the same time and the brown body tumbled backward, out of sight.

Nantana's warriors came from all sides, swarming up over the rim of the mesa while those within set up a blistering fire.

Kane's edginess went away in the action. He put all other thoughts out of his mind other than shooting as the Apache poured over the rim of the mesa, ducking and dodging, attempting to get close enough to the church wall to avoid their fire.

Some of them made it. Kane and Prince Luis looked at one another as something like a battering ram pounded on the church door.

"I'll see to it," Luis said and went swiftly down the ladder.

Finding nothing to shoot at below and hearing increased action there, Kane left the bell tower and went down the ladder to find Prince Luis firing through the huge door. Kane was halfway down when Luis jerked the door open and stepped back to fire, when suddenly he froze.

Kane watched this unfold as he hung from the ladder. The tall Apache stood in the doorway, with a look of be-

wilderment on his brown face. Prince Luis, also im-
mobilized, stood there as savage and nobleman stared at
one another, each of them with their eyes on the blue medallion around the other's neck.

Kane dropped to the floor and slammed shut the door
and dropped the bar into place. Luis turned and went
into the middle of the room, as a brown face appeared in
one of the east windows. Luis didn't act and Kane fired
his handgun and the Apache disappeared.

The charge and fight could have lasted no more than a
minute or two and it broke off suddenly and all was quiet
in the church; there was only the smell of burned gunpowder. In the distance Kane could hear the receding
whoops and barks of the Apaches.

Laxton closed in on Kane. "A glancing bullet hit the
biggest water jug," he reported. "Half our water gone in a
second."

Kane checked the others and found that Felipe had
sustained a slight wound in his right shoulder. Juanita
was staunching the flow of blood and binding it up. As
Kane stood at her shoulders, she whispered, "I fear for the
children."

"Kids are tougher than we know," Kane reassured her,
thinking of his own childhood. "They can get over these
things in time."

Luis spoke listlessly. "I must talk with Professor Flannery about all this. I—I—"

"Professor Flannery—Sean—is dead," Betty Canfield
said without emotion. "He died when the shooting
began." A tear rolled down her cheek and she touched it
with her finger and turned away.

"Where's Foulard?" Kane asked.

No one seemed to know. Kane searched the main floor
of the church and then went through the trap door and

down into the underground chamber holding a candle aloft. He found Foulard lying on the floor, clutching the haft of the halberd with its six-foot shaft sticking upright in the air. Kane pulled the halberd from Foulard's chest, noting that the lance blade had penetrated to the hook. He stood there, staring down at Foulard, with mixed emotions, one of which was regret. He should have known Giles would take the gold, and that he would kill anyone who stood in his way.

Juanita spoke from behind him. "This man Giles, he has stolen the gold, no?"

"Yes, he has taken the gold," Kane said heavily.

"Do you think he will now also go for help for us?"

"I wish I knew the answer to that," Kane said, turning and taking her arm and guiding her up the steps. "Do not tell the others of this, Juanita. It would only serve to dishearten them."

"I must learn to speak English," she said. "There are moments when I do not understand."

"There are times," Kane said, "when it is better to not understand."

Nantana waved his men away, retreating from the mesa in a state of depression. He'd seen with his own eyes the look-alike man who wore a charm exactly like the one that he hung so proudly from his own neck.

Cashis, the shaman, squatted nearby, almost as gloomy as Nantana, yet he gave no sign. In deference to the Apache leader he waited for Nantana to speak.

Nantana fingered his medallion, wanting to confide in Cashis but reluctant to do so for fear of losing face with the medicine man.

"The great Nantana is troubled," Cashis said slyly. "Things are not going as you wish."

"I can't afford to lose more warriors," Nantana said. "Yet I can't afford to not kill off these white-eyes who have so disrupted the land and our people."

"This Coyotero from the East," Cashis said craftily, "may be able to help. He knows of ways the white-eyes have of breaking up rocks without slaves."

Nantana looked at Cashis with interest. "Why would the white-eyes break up rocks?" he asked.

Cashis shrugged. "You know the white-eyes," he said. "They are all crazy and do crazy things."

"Call the Coyotero," Nantana directed, and in a few minutes the two of them were squatting, facing one another, while the Coyotero explained how the brown sticks and white fire rope worked. "It is easy," the Coyotero said. "You attach this rope to the brown sticks, make a fire at the end and when the fire reaches the brown sticks it is as though thunder and lightning such as you've never seen comes and the earth shakes. The church will fall in a ruin in an instant."

Nantana shook his head. "This I do not believe," he said.

"You'd better give it a try," Cashis said. "Time is running out for all of us."

Nantana rose. "If this is so," he said, "we'll soon rid ourselves of this pestilence and can give our attention to this man Crook and his horse soldiers."

The Coyotero nodded. "I will make it all ready," he said. "As soon as it is full dark we'll make the church disappear."

CHAPTER 20

As the day wore on, agonizingly slowly, Nantana made two half-hearted assaults and was beaten back.

"They're up to something," Kane muttered, as he walked among the defenders, bedraggled and almost ready to give up. Prince Luis' white shirt with ruffles was dirty and torn, his unshaven face darkening, becoming almost villainous. Laxton was surly and uncommunicative.

"Giles must o' got through," he said, "else the 'Paches would hold him up fer us to see, tied to a cactus, o' course."

Kane attempted to reassure them without visible effect.

Gonzales parceled out food and water in very small amounts. The women of Armijo were tough but they'd never been subjected to such as this. The center of their lives, their church, was a shambles.

Kane's heart ached for them but there was nothing he could do. Not at this moment. The woman Luz had said an Ave Maria for Foulard and Kane too wished for mercy for the man who had endured with him in his own way. Then he pushed it all from his mind and climbed to the bell tower as the sun went down in a blaze of unbelievable colors.

Laxton scrubbed a hand across his bearded face. His eyes, still discolored, were red-rimmed and watery. "We ain't gonna last much longer," he said.

"Go down and try to get some rest," Kane said. "It's going to be a long night, Laxton."

Kane sat in the tower all through the long night, wondering what Nantana was about. Kane's respect for the Apache's leadership had grown enormously in the last day or so; the knotted rawhide with which he'd tried to separate the bell tower from the church was only one example.

The eastern sky lightened, yellowed, touched with crimson. Looking off into the morning, Kane felt his heart lurch inside him. Down below, at their former campsite, Giles hung head-down from a tripod of three poles, naked, his head a few inches from a smoldering fire. The Apaches were cooking brains in a slow death.

Kane felt sickened as he flung himself down the ladder. Halfway down, he slowed, debating on what to say about this latest disaster. Hope for rescue dwindled to nothing in the space of a moment.

He called them and they gathered around him in the vestibule when it seemed as though the earth itself exploded. Kane was flung to the floor, holding Juanita. There were frightened screams of women, and the children cried aloud in fear. Dust filled the church as it seemed to fall in on itself. The door was blown open and a pile of rubble confronted them. The clangor of bells suddenly stilled.

Outside there were yells and barks, sparking Kane to action. He fumbled around, feeling for his rifle, and found nothing.

Moments after the explosion ripped the church apart, Nantana knew he had won and that he had lost. Half his band of warriors lay dead or dying. The Coyotero had done his work well, too well. Nantana had been on the eastern slope of the mesa and thus escaped, along with a handful of his braves. The bell tower had toppled into the center of the church. The west wall fell down on the campsite of the Goldhair, burying all remains of where the two men had dug into the earth, searching for gold.

Nantana slipped off his bandoleer, rid himself of all except his breechclout, leggings and spear. He stood erect and strode forward, standing a dozen feet from the ruined entrance to the church.

"I want the Goldhair," he said, "the man who killed my friend and brother, Talin. We will fight with the weapon of my fathers." He waved his lance aloft with his right hand while his left hand fingered the blue and gold medallion.

Kane's hand closed on the halberd he'd brought from the underground chamber. "Stay inside, all of you," he said, and stepped through the ruins of the door.

Maurine screamed, "You can't leave us here, Jared! There's no one but you."

Kane looked at Juanita. She was watching him and in her eyes he could see that she left the decision up to him. She was satisfied.

"Stay inside, all of you," he repeated and walked straight ahead, toward Nantana, balancing the shaft of the halberd.

Nantana crouched in fighting position, his lance at the ready. Kane paused, with the halberd at the ready.

Nantana lunged and Kane used his halberd to parry. The hook of the halberd caught on the lance and Nantana gave a savage jerk and the halberd parted just below the hook. Kane was left with a shaft in his hand, nothing more.

With a joyous gleam in his eye, Nantana leaped forward, the muscles in his arms rippling as he thrust the point of the lance toward Kane, trying for the heart.

Kane went back a step and his moccasin caught on a rock and he went down, still holding the shaft of the halberd.

"Ramon! Felipe! Do something," Juanita screamed.

"He is the patron," Felipe muttered. "He ordered us to not interfere."

"That is right, sister," Ramon agreed.

Juanita snatched Felipe's rifle from his hand and, cocking it, raised the stock to her shoulder and fired.

Nantana looked away, and Kane, now on his feet, brought the shaft of the halberd down on Nantana's head and the Apache leader fell heavily and did not move.

An eagle flew over and far down by the creek a jay screeched once and then all was silence.

Kane walked slowly around the rim of the mesa but found no sign of life. Those warriors who survived had fled.

He came back to the front of the church and found that the women and children had emerged and stood silently.

"I will build you another church," Kane promised. "I will build it closer to the village so that the elders will not have to climb this steep path to get to it."

"Ah, yes," Gonzales said, gazing forlornly at the ruined church. "You will do this, gringo, for nothing perhaps?"

Kane looked at Juanita. "For something, sir," he said.

Ramon and Felipe brought the bull-hide chair outside the ruins and Gonzales sat in it. The two brothers lifted the chair to their shoulders.

"Wait," said Kane.

The old man looked down on Kane, expectantly.

"Sir, I would like to ask the hand of your daughter in marriage."

Juanita, standing at his shoulder, opened wide her eyes in surprise.

Gonzales nodded. "It is only because there are no men in the village," he said gloomily.

"I asked a question, sir," Kane said.

"I answer," Juanita said. "Yes."

"What can I say?" Gonzales asked. "She could travel a great distance and not find such a man as you, Kane. I ask only that you treat her well and give me many grandchildren."

Kane and Juanita stood, watching the procession wind its way toward the village, Gonzales in his chair held aloft by his two burly sons, followed by the women and children.

Later that day, a flying squad from General Crook's command arrived to investigate rumors of an Apache uprising. The leathery sergeant in charge of the six enlisted men squinted at the church in disbelief, almost swallowing his tobacco cud. "Great grannies," he said. "What in tarnation happened here?"

Maurine Summers, Betty Canfield and Prince Luis emerged from the ruins of the church and approached the army men.

"I'm Maurine Summers," she said. "My father is General Summers, Secretary of War."

"Yes'm," the sergeant said. "Gen'l Crook been mighty worried 'bout you, ma'am. You ready to go?"

"Don't you want to hear about what happened?"

The sergeant shook his head. "You tell the gen'l, ma'am. My orders is to get you safe and sound back to the main body."

Maurine gave Kane a brief glance and said, "I'm—we are ready to go, Sergeant."

I 49   "You'll have to ride double 'til we get back to the column," he said and held a hand for her to mount behind him.

Prince Luis came from around the church and stood over Nantana's body. He leaned over to take the blue and gold medallion from the neck of the dead Apache leader.

"Let him keep it," Kane said.

Prince Luis straightened, his face impassive. He stood there for a moment and then came to stand before Kane. "Yes, I agree, let him keep it." He held out his hand and Kane accepted it. "I have learned much from you, Kane. Should you ever come to Spain you will be my honored guest."

"There's much to do here," Kane said. "I expect I'll not make it to your country. But thanks, anyway."

Prince Luis mounted behind a young trooper and the cavalcade moved away.

Kane and Juanita, standing close together, watched them go.

She looked up at him. "You are sure of what you are doing, Jared?"

He put his arm around her and she turned to face him, meeting her body with his. It was answer enough for both of them.